CHRISTMAS IN JUBILEE

RACHEL HANNA

2-

CHAPTER 1

Madeline couldn't believe what she was seeing. "Mom, what are you doing here?" she asked, her eyes wide.

"I came here to save you from yourself," her mother said, walking past her into the house.

She hadn't seen her mother in years. A part of her had felt guilty about that at times, but when someone was so critical of all your life choices, no matter how successful you were, you just couldn't have them in your life.

Madeline slowly closed the door and turned around to face her mother. Eloise was looking weary but determined as she stood there holding her old worn leather suitcase. Madeline had seen that suit-case many times in her life because her mother had never gotten a new one. She said that when you have something that works, you keep it. You don't need to constantly try to get the new best thing. Madeline didn't necessarily agree with that premise.

She looked at her mother in disbelief, feeling like she was seeing a mirage or maybe a nightmare. It was an awful way to feel about her own mother, but here at the beginning of fall, going into her favorite time of the year - the holiday season - Madeline couldn't believe that she was going to have her mother around. Maybe this was just going to be a quick visit. She felt a swirl of emotions in her stomach: surprise, uncertainty, and that familiar pang of dread. Why was her mother here? How did she know where Madeline even was?

She looked so different from the last time she'd seen her. Older. Grayer. More wrinkles. Thinner. Her shoulders hunching forward a bit. It made Madeline feel a sense of sadness that she couldn't quite understand.

Eloise stepped forward slightly. "Hello, Madeline? Are you not going to speak? Have you lost your ability to form words?"

Madeline hesitated a moment and then looked at her mother. "It's good to see you, Mom. Can I get you some sweet tea?" Madeline didn't know why asking if she wanted tea was her immediate reaction when seeing her mother after so many years. Maybe she was becoming more Southern living in these mountains.

Eloise stared at her and then waved a dismissive hand. "No, I don't need any tea. I'd just like to sit down, but you don't seem to be inviting me to do that."

Madeline cleared her throat and pointed toward the sofa. "Of course you can sit down. I thought that was a given."

Eloise set her suitcase behind the sofa and then walked around and sat down stiffly on the edge of the loveseat. Madeline sat at the opposite end of the sofa. Neither of them spoke as the silence swelled between them, broken only by the sound of the ticking clock on the mantle.

Finally, Madeline looked at her mother again. "So, it's been a long time. I have to say, I'm a little surprised to see you. What made you decide to visit me?"

Eloise clasped her hands tightly in her lap. "Well, I heard about the divorce and that you moved way out here in the boondocks, so I thought I needed to come out and see for myself how you're managing alone."

Madeline bristled at her mother's judgmental

tone. Some things hadn't changed. "Well, to be honest, I'm doing great," Madeline said, trying to keep her voice even. "This place has been a wonderful change for me."

Eloise pursed her lips. "Hmm, if you say so."

Madeline sighed. This was going to be a long visit. She took a deep breath and tried to keep her frustration in check. She could see her mother looking around the room with a critical eye.

"This decor is rather rustic," Eloise remarked, wrinkling her nose at the homemade quilts and bear decor lining the room. "I guess some might think it's charming, in an outdated sort of way. Are you renting it?"

"No, Mom. I bought it."

"Oh, Madeline. I don't think this was a wise investment. I hope you can get your money out of it when you sell it one day." Madeline clenched her fists, biting back sharp words that were on the tip of her tongue. She wasn't going to take the bait. "And that town. Oh, my goodness. It took me nearly two hours to get here from my house," Eloise continued with an exaggerated sigh. "The roads are dreadful. Way too curvy. And the driver I had... Well, he smelled simply awful. I had to cover my nose and crack my window." She shook her head in disapproval. "I can't imagine why anyone with half a brain would choose to live so remotely. I mean, I guess out here there are fewer distractions. It seems like there's nothing to do."

Madeline felt her face growing hotter and hotter. She opened her mouth to respond, but Eloise just continued on. “Mom, that’s not...”

"Speaking of which, what in the world do you do with yourself out here, besides read and write your stories?” She emphasized the word stories like it was a joke.

Madeline struggled to reign in her emotions. She had defended her choices so many times over the years, and she knew from experience that arguing with her mother just never got anywhere good. "I'm happy here, Mom. This is my home now." Why did she feel so powerless to speak up for herself when it came to her mother? She felt like a little child being scolded. Madeline hated who she became when her mother was around. Any other time, she was a strong, vocal woman. Until her mother appeared.

Eloise raised a skeptical eyebrow, but she seemed to momentarily accept Madeline's firm response. Then an awkward silence descended upon the room once more, like the clouds of fog that often hung above the mountains outside her window.

Madeline's cell phone suddenly buzzed beside her on the end table, causing her to jolt. She blinked a few times to clear the haze over her eyes before grabbing the phone. A slight smile spread across her face as she saw Brady's name on the screen. She quickly read the message. *"Thinking of you. Can't wait to see you soon."* Warmth spread across her chest as she typed out a quick reply and then put her phone face down on the coffee table in front of her.

"Who was that?" Eloise asked. “Your face blushed when you read it.”

Madeline hesitated, suddenly feeling like a self-conscious teenager. “Just a friend."

Eloise's eyes narrowed, Madeline could see a judgmental response forming on her lips. She braced herself for the inevitable criticism about her life and her choices, but Eloise just pursed her lips and gave a curt nod. "I see. Well, I'm feeling a bit tired from my travels. Can you show me where I'll be staying?"

Suddenly Madeline realized her mother was planning to stay there. In her home. She wasn't going to a hotel. She wasn't going to the inn. She was staying at her house.

"Of course. Follow me." Madeline stood and led her mother down a short hallway to the guest bedroom. She was thankful that she would soon be able to close the door on the woman who had made her feel self-conscious for much of her life. She was going to need that door between them to keep her sanity intact for this visit.

She opened the door to the guest room, with its log walls and rustic decor. The bed was queen-sized and made out of logs as well. Eloise set her suitcase on the bed, and then Madeline could see her scanning the room looking for flaws.

"Well, it's a bit smaller than what I'm accustomed to, but I guess it will do."

Madeline bit her tongue, worried that blood was literally going to come out of her mouth at any moment. "Well, I'm glad it's okay for you. Let me know if you need anything else." She turned to leave, eager to escape to her own bedroom.

"Just a moment. Come sit with me." Madeline hesitated, but then reluctantly sat on the edge of the bed beside her mother, bracing herself for whatever was coming next. "I know things have been difficult between us," Eloise began, "but I want you to know that I'm here because I do care about you. I am your mother, after all. I would like for us to try to repair our relationship." Madeline nodded slightly. She wanted that too, but she had wanted that many times in her life, and it had never worked out. She learned to never trust her mother's intentions or her words.

"I would like that, too."

"You ended your marriage so abruptly, and then you disappeared to this remote town. I'm worried about what's going on with you. I think maybe you could have reconciled with your husband if you had tried harder."

The words slammed into Madeline like her mother had punched her in the face. Her throat constricted, and she moved further away on the bed. "There was nothing I could have done. He made his choice when he destroyed our wedding vows, and I won't apologize for choosing myself. Surely, *you* of all people can understand that." Eloise didn't like to talk about Madeline's father leaving the family and never looking back.

Her mother looked at her, taken aback. "Have you ever thought that maybe your husband made that choice because you were never around? You were always at book signings. I saw them on the Internet."

"So, because I did well at my job, my husband had the right to cheat on me with my best friend?"

Eloise rolled her eyes. "Madeline, you've always

been so dramatic. I guess that's why you make up stories and write them for other people to read. It has been quite embarrassing, I have to say."

"Embarrassing? What is that supposed to mean?" Madeline said, standing up.

"It just means that some of my friends have picked up your books, and it's embarrassing to think this is what my daughter does for a living. That you just talk to imaginary friends in your head and write it down. What an odd career choice for someone."

"So you think people shouldn't write books. Is that what you're saying? Because that sounds crazy, Mom. If that's the case, the entire fiction world shouldn't exist, in your eyes."

"I'm not saying I don't like literature. Romance books are, well, silly as far as I'm concerned. I'm just saying, now that you have this second chance in life, maybe you should try a new career field."

"You know what? I'm hungry. I'm going to go make dinner. I'll let you know when it's ready," Madeline said, walking out of the room and slamming the door behind her.

She walked into the kitchen and leaned against one of the counters, taking in a deep breath and blowing it out as slowly as she could. Just like she'd been taught in yoga class many times. How was she going to do this? Maybe she should tell her mother she wasn't welcome there, that she needed to go stay at the inn, or at a local hotel, or just go back to her own home. But being the only child and knowing that her mother was getting older, Madeline felt responsible. Just like Brady was responsible for his sister and niece, Madeline had a responsibility to her mother, or at least that's what she thought.

As she busied herself in the kitchen, trying to create a simple meal that they could both eat, Madeline thought about all the times that she had hoped that she and her mother would be able to put things back together. But it seemed that her mother was never able to change. She was never able to see the point of Madeline's work. And because writing books was the biggest part of her life, she couldn't have a relationship with someone who thought her life's work was silly.

She continued making pasta with some homemade tomato basil sauce she had in the refrigerator. She also made a side salad and put some garlic bread in the toaster.

As her mind wandered while she was chopping vegetables for the salad, she thought about Jacob. She thought about all the years that she was unhappy, but didn't know how to get out of it. And how relieved she was when he actually cheated on her. As painful as it was, it was like her ticket out of a place she knew she shouldn't be. And now that she had met Brady, she knew that he was her soulmate. For the first time in years, she felt open to possibilities.

When dinner was done, she lightly tapped on her mother's door and told her it was ready. She made herself a plate and went and sat down at the table. Eloise came out of her room and made a plate as well, sitting across from her.

"Well, it smells good," Eloise said as she sat down.

"Thanks. I hope you like it," Madeline said with no emotion.

They ate in silence until after a few bites Eloise put her fork down. "I don't mean to be harsh," she started. Madeline knew that she *did* mean to be harsh. She always did. "But if you'd had kids to take care of instead of being so career focused, you would know how to cook a proper meal."

Madeline froze, her fork hovering above her plate. "I happen to think this is a pretty good meal, especially for someone who would be going hungry right now because she apparently didn't plan to let her daughter know that she was arriving."

Eloise looked back down at her food and said nothing, taking another bite. And that was how the first night of her visit went.

It had been a long time since Frannie had been back to Jubilee. As she drove down Main Street, the familiar storefronts slid by in a blur. She would visit them soon, but right now she needed to get to her Nana's house. She gripped her steering wheel tighter as her stomach clenched with apprehension and nostalgia. She saw the hardware store, the pharmacy, her favorite eateries. She saw the coffee shop and the bookstore, both places that she planned to visit as soon as she could. Everything seemed to be frozen in time, much unchanged since her childhood summers that she spent here with her beloved Nana.

As the years had passed, she had come to Jubilee less and less. First, she became a teenager and didn't want to visit her grandmother as often as she should have. Then there was college, an ill-fated marriage, and a career that kept her away. Now her Nana was gone. It was something she hadn't quite come to terms with, and she knew she would miss her forever.

Her grandmother had been a constant source of support and inspiration in her life since she was a child. She didn't remember a life without Nana, and now here she was, about to pull up to her house, this place that she had inherited and that had all the memories of her childhood wrapped up inside of it. She couldn't believe she was going to own her Nana's house. Frannie had lost her own mother seven years ago, and she was the next in line to inherit the place that had held all of her family's legacy for as long as she could remember.

Her grandmother had asked to be cremated and have some of her ashes spread on the property. She didn't want a memorial service. She just wanted to slip quietly into heaven, so Frannie had honored that decision. She would soon pick up her urn from the funeral home, along with some ashes she could spread.

As she pulled up to the pale-yellow farmhouse, she let out a long breath. Her favorite part of the place were the rolling green hills that stretched for acres behind the property. Her grandmother had told her as a child that they were called "frolicking hills." Later, Frannie realized that was just something her grandmother made up to get her to go run out on the property and wear herself out. The thought of it made her smile now.

"Child, those hills were made for frolicking! If you don't do it, who will?" her Nana would say, swatting at her rear end until she ran outside and burned off her energy.

The place definitely needed some work. In later years, her grandmother had struggled with health problems. Thankfully, she had been able to get home healthcare arranged for her so that Nana could stay in her home until the very end. Frannie had tried to get there before she passed away, but unfortunately she didn't make it in time. Her second cousin, Cecilia, had been able to travel to town to be with her so she wasn't alone. Frannie tried not to think about those last moments.

As she stepped out of the car and up onto the creaking porch, she smiled again, remembering each one that had always made that sound. The creaking sound was like its own special music that went with the property. She knew that the floorboards needed to be fixed as they were starting to sag under her feet and dust was coating every surface, but it felt wrong to replace boards that wouldn't sing as she walked across them.

"Oh, Nana," she murmured to herself, running her finger over the dusty piano as she walked into the house. It left a clean streak across the dark wood. She remembered all the times that her grandmother would sit behind the keys, playing her favorite church hymns and Christmas songs during the holidays. Sometimes, they would stand next to her and sing. Those were good memories. She could almost hear the music swirling through the air.

As she swallowed a lump in her throat, she walked through each dusty room with memories flooding back in each one. In the kitchen, she even found a jar of chocolate chip cookies that they used to bake together. Of course, they were old now, with a spider inhabiting the clear glass container. She would have to get rid of that immediately. She wondered when her grandmother made these cookies. Given her health issues, she didn't know how she would've done it. Maybe her caregiver made them. Frannie would never know.

She wiped away a stray tear that rolled down her cheek and whispered to her grandmother's spirit, "Don't worry, Nana, I will make this place shine again just like you did." Her grandmother had been a clean freak and Frannie was very much the opposite. She was somebody who liked to keep every little thing and had all sorts of collections. Now an adult, she tried really hard not to do that, but it was a challenge that she had to work at every single day. Nana, on the other hand, cleaned and cleaned until her hands were raw. She never let dust make an appearance in her house, so it was very sad for Frannie to see the state it was in.

Nana had passed away weeks ago, and Frannie was only just now getting back to Jubilee. Her job as a nurse at a hospital near Atlanta was challenging, and she had moved her way up in her career over the last few years. Now she wished that she had spent more time in Jubilee, more time with her grandmother. But there would never have been enough time.

Madeline couldn't take it anymore. She felt the tension in her home like a thick fog after each interaction with her mother. She needed clarity, and she knew she wasn't going to find it within the four walls of her cabin right now.

She slipped into her boots and zipped up her jacket before stepping out into the crisp fall air, letting the door close softly behind her. Her mother had said she wanted to go lie down for a while, so she was hoping she was asleep and wouldn't notice that Madeline was gone.

She walked aimlessly down the gravel road that led away from her home, her boots crunching against the fallen leaves. Her thoughts were swirling, each one pulling her deeper into a sea of confusion and doubt. Why had her mother even come to Jubilee, and why did every single conversation they had feel like a razor blade against her skin?

Lost in her thoughts, she almost missed seeing Geneva standing in her yard. She had been pulling weeds from her flower bed. Looking up, her eyes met Madeline's, a warm smile spreading across her face.

"What in the world is going on? I never see you out here taking a walk."

Madeline laughed as she moved closer to Geneva. "I guess you could say I just needed a little break. I see you're working hard."

Geneva chuckled as she brushed the dirt off her knees. "Well, these old flowerbeds won't tend to themselves. Come over here and have a seat with me for a minute." She pointed at the wooden bench that was on the edge of her porch. Madeline walked over and sat down beside her.

"Is it that obvious that I need somebody to talk to?"

Geneva's eyes were filled with wisdom that only years of living could bring. "Well, when you've been around as long as I have, you learn to read people. And right now you're an open book."

Madeline sighed, her shoulders dropping. "It's my mother, Geneva. She's here, and I don't know how to handle it. I think I've told you that our relationship has always been so complicated."

Geneva looked at her, her eyes soft. "You know, relationships with mothers often are. Remember, we can't control somebody else's actions. We can only control our reaction to them."

"But how do I react to someone who has always been so critical?"

"Now, you told me that when you were little, you were close to your mother, right?"

"Yeah, pretty much. Until my father left, and then things just seemed to fall apart. She's become so much more negative and critical, and I see that nothing has changed. I had to eventually put up boundaries and stop interacting with her.

"And that's understandable, Madeline. You had to protect yourself, but maybe your mother is here because she wants to reconnect with you."

"I want to hope that's true, but I just have this nagging feeling that there's something else I'm missing. Some other little surprise she has in store for me."

"Well, you can't really do anything about that. Maybe you're just dreaming up terrible scenarios in your head, and for good reason. But you have to give her a chance, don't you?"

"I don't know. Do I?" Madeline asked, confused.

"Well, it seems to me you have two choices here. You can let her criticisms define you, or you can let it refine you. You can become bitter, or you can become better."

Madeline giggled. "Did you read that off a bumper sticker?"

"Sayings become popular because they're good. They have meaning."

"I don't know, Geneva. Part of me says that I should just tell my mom to get her suitcase and leave, that this is going nowhere good."

"But here's the problem, dear. Won't you always wonder what could have been if you send your mom on her way, especially at the holidays? If I know you, Madeline, you're not going to be okay with yourself in your heart or in your soul if you send your mother away right now."

Madeline thought for a long moment. "I know you're right. I just hate not knowing what she's up to."

"I will say this because I'm about your mother's age, I would think. Sometimes we get to this stage of life, and we look back and see all the mistakes that we made. And sometimes we're brave enough to try to make them right. Sometimes people go to their graves without ever making anything right. So, if it's possible, just give your mom a little bit of grace and try to understand that she's in the golden years of her life. Maybe she's just trying to make things good again."

Madeline felt tears welling up in her eyes. Maybe Geneva was right. Maybe her mother, in her own weird and often warped way, was trying to repair the damage to their relationship. She had a funny method of going about it, but Madeline had to believe there was some point to all of this.

"What if I'm not strong enough to deal with this?"

Geneva reached over and took her hand, her grip firm, yet gentle. "Strength isn't a solitary thing, dear. You have a community here. You have friends, a loving boyfriend, people who see the beauty in you, even when you don't see it in yourself. You're not alone anymore. Lean on all of us."

Madeline felt a tear escape, rolling down her cheek. "Thank you, Geneva. I don't know what I would do without you."

Geneva squeezed her hand. "You'll never have to find out."

As Madeline stood and started walking back toward her house, she felt a newfound sense of resolve within her. She was going to figure out how to coexist with her mother no matter what it took. She knew there were going to be challenges, but at least she didn't have to face them alone, and for some reason that made all the difference.

CHAPTER 2

Madeline opened her eyes to the sound of the crows squawking just outside her window. It was one of the things that she'd had to get used to after moving to Jubilee. Living out basically in the middle of the national forest meant she heard all kinds of birds and other critters that she had never heard before in her life. But it was starting to grow on her, at least most of the time.

She yawned and stretched her arms high above her head, wiggling down under the covers a little further. Surely it was a nightmare that her mother had shown up at her door yesterday and she was definitely *not* just right downstairs sleeping in the guest room beneath her. That had to have been a bad dream. It made her feel guilty to think so.

As she wiped the sleep out of her eyes, she realized that it wasn't a dream. Her mother was definitely downstairs, and she didn't know what she was going to do with her. She was one of the most difficult people she'd ever had to deal with, and it was sad, really, because when she was growing up, Madeline was quite close to her mother. It was only after her father left for another woman that her mother's attitude seemed to change. She seemed to become a more negative person. Pessimistic. Critical. Madeline didn't know what caused that, but after a while she just couldn't deal with it anymore. And as an adult, she created boundaries that she had stuck to for many years now.

She sat up and swung her legs around to the side of the bed, trying to get her bearings before she stood. Madeline tended toward low blood pressure, which was hysterical since she was a high-stress kind of person. She tried not to stand up too quickly, especially in the mornings before she had her big glass of water that she had started drinking to combat the problem.

She sat there for a moment and thought about her friends and coworkers back in Atlanta who had good relationships with their mothers. There were times that she would hear about weekend shopping trips or mother-daughter vacations and wish that she had that kind of connection with her own mother. Maybe it was partially her fault for not trying harder, but how hard was a person supposed to try when they were constantly getting criticized?

Madeline had always wanted to make her mother proud, and even in her mid fifties, she still had that small part of her that wanted to do that. But, it seemed like Eloise couldn't be made happy. She couldn't be proud of her only daughter for her success, and Madeline would never understand why. Even though she wasn't a mother herself, she did not think she would have treated her own daughter that way.

She stood up and put on her slippers, turning to walk toward the bathroom when she heard her cell phone ringing on the nightstand. "Who in the world is calling this early in the morning?" she said to herself. Living alone, she found that she talked to herself quite a bit. She had considered getting a dog, but since she'd never had one in her life, she wasn't sure if she was cut out for pet ownership. She did have a bird one time, but she accidentally let it go when she was cleaning its cage one day outside. It was a stupid decision, but she always wished and hoped that the bird had a happy life flying free. It was unlikely, but that was how she liked to think about it.

"Hello?" she answered, kind of irritated and assuming it was a spammer. Instead, Clemmy spoke from the other end of the phone.

"I hope it's not too early," she said in her normal chipper voice.

"No, no, it's fine. What can I help you with?"

"Well, I wanted to talk to you about the upcoming harvest festival. You know it's just in a couple of weeks."

"Oh, I think I saw a flyer for that. I don't know much about it."

"Well, I was hoping that you would help me organize it," Clemmy said, obviously hoping that Madeline was going to say yes.

"Me? Why would you ask me to help you organize it?"

"Well, I assume as an author that you have to do a lot of plotting and organizing of your book before you write it. You seemed like one of the most likely candidates."

"I don't know, Clemmy. I don't think I would be very good at that. I've never even been to a harvest festival, much less planned one."

"Well, there's a first time for everything."

"Listen, I've got a lot going on right now. My mom showed up randomly at my house yesterday, and I'm still trying to figure out why."

"That's wonderful, Madeline. I'm sure you're excited to show your mom your new hometown."

Madeline paused for a long moment. "Well, we don't exactly have the best relationship."

"Oh, I'm so sorry to hear that. Is there anything I can do?"

"No, it's just a personality conflict, I guess you would say. I haven't seen her in years. I haven't spoken to her in a long time. But she just showed up at my door yesterday. It was kind of weird."

"Where is she now?"

"She's asleep in the guest room below me," Madeline said, keeping her voice as low as possible. She opened up the door leading out to her porch so she could get a little more privacy.

"So, what are you going to do?" Clemmy asked.

"Well, I don't know. She's somebody I don't get along with very well, to put it bluntly. She's very critical, and I can't have that in my life. I put up boundaries a long time ago."

Clemmy paused for a long moment, obviously trying to be careful with her words. "I don't want to step on your toes, honey. I know we don't know each other all that well yet, but I'm ten years older than you, and I feel like I can give you a little bit of advice."

"I always appreciate wise advice," Madeline said, not really wanting to hear it this early in the morning but trying to be polite, nonetheless.

"I lost my mom about twenty years ago."

"Oh, Clemmy, I'm so sorry to hear that."

"We had a wonderful relationship, very close, and I'm thankful for that. But we had our moments, as mothers and daughters often do. What I can tell you from experience is that no matter what kind of relationship you have with your mother, when she's gone, you're going to feel a kind of pain that's hard to explain to anyone who hasn't gone through it."

"I can't imagine." Madeline had wondered about that over the years. When her mother was gone, was she going to feel anything? Was it going to be painful? Would she grieve? She felt like she would, but maybe more so for the relationship that she wished she'd had with her mother, rather than the woman herself. After all, she hadn't seen her or spoken to her for years, and it was something she still felt guilty about even though she knew she shouldn't. She had just been protecting herself, or maybe not wanting to deal with the hard challenge of repairing a relationship when only one person was interested in doing it.

"I miss my mother every day," Clemmy said. Madeline could hear her voice choking up. "But that's not what this is about. I just want to warn you to not give up so soon or so easily. People are weird and quirky. They have their own issues, and I bet your mom's critical nature comes from somewhere. Perhaps from something that has caused her pain. And maybe if you can get to that, you can get to healing in your relationship."

"I appreciate the advice. I'm going to do my best. I don't know how long she's planning to stay or why she's really here, but I intend to find out."

"Well, back to my original point of this call. A great way to distract yourself from this is to help me plan the festival," Clemmy said, laughing.

Madeline couldn't help but giggle. "You would have made a great saleswoman."

Clemmy laughed. "I am a great saleswoman. I own a bookstore, remember?"

"Okay, okay. I'll help you. I'm not sure how much help I'll be, but I will show up and do what you need me to do."

"Wonderful. That is so exciting to hear. Maybe we can meet for lunch in a few days?"

"Sure, that sounds great."

"Okay. I'll text you when I can look at my schedule. Thanks again, Madeline, and good luck with your mom."

Madeline chuckled. "Thank you. I have a feeling I'm going to need it."

Madeline took a quick shower and got ready for the day, taking her time before she walked downstairs to interact with her mother. A good night of sleep had helped her, certainly, but she didn't know what the days and weeks to come were going to hold. Was her mother planning on staying for an extended time? Was she only planning to stay a couple of days and then head back out of town? Madeline didn't know what to think because they really hadn't had a conversation about it.

She walked out of her bedroom, and as she made her way to the small landing outside of her bedroom door, the smell overwhelmed her. She felt like she was back in her childhood, suddenly. She could hear the crackle of bacon and smell the pancake batter wafting through the air. She walked downstairs to see her mother standing in the kitchen wearing

Madeline's apron, finishing up some scrambled eggs on the stovetop.

She didn't make her presence known for a moment as she watched her mother work. She remembered those wonderful days when her parents were happy and Madeline enjoyed being a part of her family, back before her mother became so critical and negative. She wondered what the change was and what had caused it, but right now, her stomach was growling so much that she couldn't think very deep thoughts.

"Good morning," Madeline said. Eloise put her hand on her chest and turned around, obviously startled.

"You scared me to death."

"Sorry, I thought you heard me," Madeline said.

"Well, I didn't. My hearing's not what it used to be. I thought I'd cook us a nice breakfast this morning. It's always good to have a proper meal first thing in the day," Eloise said, taking two plates out of the cabinet.

She seemed to have made herself at home in the kitchen, which was fine because Madeline didn't love to cook like her mother did. She would give her that. She was a good cook, always had been. She remembered the many meals they ate throughout her life. Eloise had taken every cooking class she could find and had more recipe books than Madeline had ever seen. She had never been an overly southern style of cook. She liked to cook fancier things from different parts of the world where she said she would never visit because she wasn't leaving America.

"Thanks for cooking. It smells great," Madeline said, walking over and sitting down at the table. Her mother made her a plate and poured a glass of orange juice and a cup of coffee, putting it on the table in front of her.

"Cream and sugar?"

"Always," Madeline said laughing. This small moment with her mother was something she hadn't expected. She couldn't look past all the criticisms and harsh words, but right now, she was thankful for just this one little moment in time. Sometimes you had to take what you could get.

Eloise made her own plate and sat down across from her daughter looking past her at the window overlooking the mountains. "It's a beautiful view."

Madeline turned around slightly and looked at it. "Yes, it is. I feel very lucky to wake up every morning and see that."

"Still, I think I would prefer a beach view," Eloise

said. Ah, yes, a wonderful start to the day. The first criticism. "So what are your plans for the day?”

"Well, I need to get some writing done on a book I'm working on. I have to turn it into my publisher in a few weeks."

"Another book," Eloise said, laughing under her breath.

"And why is that funny?"

"I'm just wondering how many you're going to write. Is this what you're planning to do for the rest of your life?"

"Mom, it's my career. You wouldn't ask me that if I was a nurse or an accountant. Why is it so strange that I'm a novelist?"

"Not strange. Just wondering if it's what you plan to do with the rest of your life," Eloise asked, taking a bite of scrambled eggs. "I mean, don't you have any other aspirations?"

"No, I don't. I aspire to be happy. I aspire to be successful. That's really it, and that's okay."

"All right, dear. I don't want to start an argument. That's not why I came here."

"Then maybe you should stop saying hurtful things."

Eloise put down her fork and stared at Madeline. "Hurtful things? What have I said that's so hurtful?"

“Just about everything you've said since you arrived on my front porch has been hurtful. You've judged the decor, the town, the roads, my career," Madeline said staring at her as she emphasized the word career.

"I'm not judging or being critical. I'm just your mother, and I'm supposed to give you input."

"I'm fifty-five years old, Mom. I don't need your input. In fact, let's make a new rule. If I need your input, I'll ask for it."

Eloise stared at her with her mouth hanging open. Madeline had never spoken to her that way before, even though she'd felt like doing it many times.

"Excuse me?"

"The reason why we haven't had a relationship in so many years is because of the way that you talk to me. I don't like feeling judged, so I had to put up boundaries."

Eloise rolled her eyes. "Boundaries. Your generation has all of these fancy words."

"Okay, well call it whatever you want, but you're not going to come here and talk negatively about my life."

"Fine. I'll try to do better," Eloise said before going back to her plate. Madeline wondered what her angle was. What was she doing here? There had to be some reason why she had just suddenly arrived in Jubilee, especially since she didn't seem to like the place.

Before they could continue their conversation, there was a tap at the door. Madeline looked up and could see Brady standing there through the glass. Oh, no. She had wanted time to explain to him that her mother was there, but she'd been so tired after yesterday that she didn't even text him more than to say goodnight.

She was planning to go to his house today and explain the whole thing. Of course, she had talked to Brady a bit about her relationship with her mother, but he hadn't seen it firsthand, and she was afraid of what he was going to think when he did. He had been close to his parents and grandparents.

"Who is that," Eloise asked, craning her head toward the door.

"Stay here. I'll be right back." Madeline got up and walked to the front door, slipping outside onto the porch and pushing Brady sideways.

"Good morning," Brady said laughing as she pushed him down the porch. "What's going on? Is there somebody in there?"

Madeline put her hands on his chest and stared

up at him. "My mother showed up on my front porch yesterday out of the blue."

"Your mother? Didn't you tell me you haven't talked to her in years?"

"Yes. I don't even really know why she's here yet, but it has been a very stressful twelve hours."

"Oh, Madeline, I'm so sorry. Is there anything I can do?"

"Maybe take me away. I was thinking Italy? Iceland?"

Brady laughed. "I don't think that's the answer to your problem. Why don't you just ask your mom why she's here?"

"Because she's not going to tell me the truth. She's telling me that she is worried about the fact that I've moved out here to the boondocks and that she wants to repair our relationship. But so far, all she's done is criticize me, this town, and the cabin. I don't need you to be added to that list."

"You're saying you don't want me to meet your mom?"

"I don't think now is the time, Brady."

"Well, it seems my daughter is not being very polite by inviting you in," Eloise said stepping out of the door. Madeline knew they should have run and hidden behind his truck.

"Hi, I'm Brady Nolan." Brady walked toward Eloise with his hand out. She begrudgingly shook it.

"And how do you know my daughter?"

"Well, I'm her neighbor. I live down at the corner. I run a little farm."

"A farmer. Wonderful," Eloise said under her breath.

"Mom, you're being very rude," Madeline said, walking over.

Brady looked at her. "It's okay," he whispered.

"I'm not trying to be rude. Farmers run the country. How else would we eat?" Eloise said, forcing a smile.

"I agree, but I'm not a farmer. I just own a small farm."

"I'm not sure I understand the difference," Eloise said, looking over at Madeline.

"Brady has a farm where he helps rehabilitate animals. He also does contracting work, and he's a volunteer firefighter." For some reason she felt like she had to defend him.

"Interesting," Eloise said. "Well, I have a wonderful breakfast prepared inside. Would you like to join us, Brady?"

Madeline secretly hoped that Brady would say

no, that he was too busy, that he didn't have time to come inside, but instead he smiled and said, "Sure."

They all walked inside, and Eloise made Brady a plate and patted for him to sit down next to her. Madeline wanted to crawl under the table. This wasn't going to go well.

"So, how long have you lived here, Brady?"

"Oh, pretty much my whole life since I was a little kid. We lived one town over when I was young."

"And you plan to stay here for the rest of your life?"

Brady chuckled. "I hope so. I'd love to be blessed enough to do that."

"I suppose there are a lot of people that love to live here," Eloise said, taking a bite of her pancakes.

"Yes ma'am. This is God's country."

“I’m not sure I know what that means.” For once, she seemed genuinely interested in Brady’s answer.

“Look out there,” Brady said, pointing to the mountains that stretched across all of Madeline’s windows. “This place is a sanctuary, untouched and pure. It’s a place where you can feel like you’re a part of something so much greater than yourself. To me, this isn’t just land. It’s the place where I find peace, where my soul feels at home. Every time I see a sunset, or I hear the wind whisper through the towering pine trees, I am reminded that some things are just too beautiful to be accidental and have to be divine. Just like your daughter," he added, winking at Madeline.

Eloise stared at him for a long moment. "Wow. A farmer and a poet, it seems."

Madeline wanted to crawl under the table. "I'm sorry," she mouthed to Brady while her mother was focused on her plate again. He smiled and waved his hand.

"How long do you plan to stay in Jubilee?" he asked, unbothered.

Eloise shrugged her shoulders. "Oh, I don't know. I'm just taking it day by day, I suppose."

"Well, I hope you fall in love with our little town and decide to stay a good long time."

She scoffed. "Highly doubtful, but stranger things have happened."

"Some of them have happened at this very table," Madeline grumbled before stuffing her mouth with pancake.

CHAPTER 3

After a good night of sleep, Frannie woke up the next morning ready to work. She had to get her grandmother's house back in order. Whether she ended up staying in Jubilee permanently or selling the house and going back home, she still needed to get the place in good order.

There was a part of her that felt pulled back to Jubilee, the place where she'd spent so many summers and holidays with her beloved grandmother. Although she had never lived there full time - except during a short time in high school - she'd made a lot of friends in Jubilee over the years. There were still a lot of her grandmother's friends in town, and these were the women that she felt drawn to. She would go visit them as soon as she could, but for now, she had to get the house in order.

There was a lot of cleaning to be done and maybe even some repairs. She rolled up her sleeves and got to work, starting to wipe away the years of dust and grime. She scrubbed down the kitchen counters, got on her knees and wiped the floors, and cleaned the windows until they sparkled like brand new.

Hours and hours went by as she hummed softly, feeling her grandmother's presence in the home. Frannie didn't like to clean. She was unsure of why anybody would enjoy something like that, but because she was in her grandmother's home, she felt connected to her. She could have cleaned for days if she'd needed to.

When she finally made it to her grandmother's small study, she ran her fingers across the bookcase full of books her grandmother loved to read. She would read anything from romance or historical novels to cookbooks. She had all kinds of religious books as well, including the Bible that Frannie had seen her carry for decades. It was well-worn with lots of notes inside, and Frannie was so happy to see it again. She was afraid something might've happened to it over the years. She took it off the bookcase and sat down in her grandmother's over-stuffed armchair. It had a small hole in one of the arms that her Nana had tried to fix with fabric tape at one point.

She opened the Bible and saw her grandmother's handwriting, which brought back a flurry of memories. All the birthday cards and letters her grandmother had written her over the years. Each of them always smelled like her Nana's perfume with a hint of jasmine.

As she opened to the middle of the Bible, she suddenly saw an envelope overstuffed and sealed with her name on it. Her breath caught in her throat when she saw her name. Of course, the attorney had read her will and Frannie had been gifted the house and all the contents given that she was her grandmother's closest living relative, but she didn't know what this was about.

She took in a deep breath and prepared herself for what was to come. She had no idea what her grandmother would say in the letter. Maybe she would tell her how proud she was of her and how much she loved her, but maybe she would tell her how disappointed she was that she hadn't visited more as she got older.

Frannie slowly opened the envelope and realized that the stack of papers was her grandmother's recipes. One of the things her grandmother loved to do was bake. She baked everything from pound cakes to birthday cakes, and Frannie had loved watching her do it. As far as she was concerned, there was nobody who was a better cook or a better baker than her Nana.

She sorted through the recipes, smiling as she looked at each one and remembering all the family events they'd had over the years. Even the recipe for her grandmother's fruitcake was in there. Most people didn't care for fruitcake and Frannie agreed, but her grandmother had a special recipe that tasted like heaven itself. She couldn't wait to make that one during the holiday season.

Sometimes she was sad when she thought about the fact that she was divorced with no kids and had no memories to make during the holidays like she did when she was younger. She had always intended to be a mom and have a bunch of kids underfoot until they all left home and went off to college or got married.

Instead, she was in her thirties, unmarried with no kids. She didn't even have a pet right now. Life was feeling a little lonely as the holiday season was approaching. And now sitting in her grandmother's house without her, she felt a tear roll down her cheek. It was all just too much.

Holding these recipes was like holding her family legacy, but yet she had no one to pass them on to. She had no family. Her grandmother had been all she had, and now she was gone. The weight of the grief started to overwhelm her as she wiped away the tears now streaming from her eyes. Once she got herself together, she looked back at the recipes, carefully turning the fragile pages. Her grandmother's loopy cursive writing made her smile. It was from a time gone by when people still wrote in cursive.

As she looked at the last recipe, which was her grandmother's famous chocolate chip cookies, she noticed a piece of paper with her name on it. She opened it with trembling fingers and started to read the letter her grandmother had written to her. She didn't know how long ago she'd written it, but it didn't matter. Frannie started to read and feel her grandmother's presence in the process.

My dearest Frannie,

If you're reading this letter, it's because I've gone home to live with God. I left you the house because I know that you'll find happiness here in Jubilee. In the recent past, your life has been in a bit of upheaval, and I know it's hard to start over. We've all had to start over in our lives, and I know you'll be just fine.

Tears started to blur the words for Frannie as she read. This must have been more recently, maybe during her divorce. Her grandmother understood after losing her first husband. She knew what it was like for a woman to have to start over, although in her time, it would've been a lot more difficult. She continued reading the letter.

You know one of my biggest dreams was to open a bakery. That was something that you and I shared. I have a special surprise for you. I hope you look at it as a blessing. Although this is all in my will, I asked my attorney not to read this part to you because I wanted it to be more of a surprise when you found these recipes. I knew you'd look for my Bible when you wanted to feel close to me, my dear Frannie.

I rented a space on the town square for many years, as you know. I ran my sewing and alterations business, and boy did I sew up a storm for the people of Jubilee over those years. But then I got older, and I wasn't able to keep it open anymore, so it's been sitting vacant.

My dear friend owned the space and just couldn't bear to rent it out to someone else. She always thought that maybe I would somehow come back and finally open that bakery. A few months ago, she sold me that space for a very good price that I couldn't pass up. So, if there seems to be a little less in my savings account than you were anticipating, it's because I now own that space on the square.

I got to stake my claim in Jubilee and, as a woman, that was a real accomplishment for me. Things were different in my time, and I was very proud to sign those papers and call that space mine.

I never got to open my bakery, Frannie, and I think you'd be just the person to do it for me.

Frannie clutched the letter tighter, almost ripping the paper.

I love you, and I know that you'll miss me. I'll miss you, too, but I'll always be there. I'll be there in my home, in the rolling hills behind it, and I'll be there on the day that you open that brand new bakery on the square of Jubilee. In every cookie and cake, I'll be there in spirit, cheering you on from afar.

Love, Nana

Frannie pulled the letter to her chest, tears streaming down her face, yet again.

"I'm home. Nana," she said to herself. "I'll make your dream come true." She closed her eyes and pictured the bakery in her mind. The display cases filled with all kinds of delicious treats. The cash register ringing, the scent of baked goods wafting out onto the street and drawing people inside.

Suddenly, her heart swelled with a purpose.

Jubilee was where she belonged, and she was going to make a new life here.

The bell above the door jingled as Frannie entered Perky's Coffee Shop, one of her favorite places in Jubilee. She inhaled the rich aroma of the roasted coffee beans and breathed in all the memories she'd had there over the years. Perky had been like a second grandmother to her. She'd known her for her entire life. As she saw her behind the counter with her dyed black bouffant hairdo and her blue eyeshadow, Frannie knew she was home. She couldn't help but smile when she saw her.

"Well, look what the cat dragged in," Perky bellowed as she smiled and waved. Frannie grinned as Perky pulled her into a warm hug. It had been a long time since she had seen her last, but her grandmother's best friend hadn't changed a bit. Her eyes crinkled in delight behind wire-rimmed glasses.

"It is so great to see you, Perky," Frannie said. "This place never changes."

Perky giggled. "Well, if it ain't broke, don't fix it. That's what I think. Come on over here and have a seat. I just baked a fresh batch of my snickerdoodles." Although Perky was mostly interested in selling coffee, she did have a few baked goods. Frannie was hoping that she wouldn't be offended when she opened a bakery just a few doors down from the coffee shop.

Perky walked behind the counter and then reappeared with a snickerdoodle wrapped in a piece of wax paper and set it in front of Frannie. She didn't have the heart to tell her that she was trying to lose some weight and really didn't need to be eating this kind of thing. Of course, if she opened a bakery herself, she was probably going to be sampling a lot of high-calorie foods in the very near future.

"This is delicious as always," Frannie said, smiling as she took her first bite. It brought back so many happy memories of baking with her grandmother and Perky over the years.

"There's no need to change a recipe that's perfect. You know I got that recipe from your grandmother originally, but I always told her I made it up myself. We fought about that many times," she said, laughing.

"It's so good to be back here. Nothing has really changed in Jubilee from what I can see."

"We like to keep it that way," Perky said, slapping her on the hand playfully.

“Listen, I wanted to talk to you about something," Frannie started.

"Okay. What's going on, sugar?"

"Well, I went to Nana's house and started cleaning it out. It's been a lot of work, as you can imagine."

"Yeah. That place has fallen into disrepair over the years," Perky said. "I thought many times about going over there myself, but my joints aren't what they used to be."

"It wasn't your job, Perky. My nana wanted me to do it, and I was happy to. It was the least I could do, especially since she left me the house."

“I'm so tickled pink that she left you that house, dear. That's exactly where it should have gone.”

"And I've decided to stay in Jubilee."

Perky's eyes widened. "Really? That's wonderful. I can't wait to have you around town more. What are you planning to do here?"

"Well, that's just it. I was going through some of my Nana's things, and I came across an envelope filled with her recipes."

"Really? That's fantastic. I hoped that they wouldn't get lost in all of this. Your grandmother was the best baker I've ever known."

"I agree. It had everything in it, including a letter to me."

"A letter?"

"Apparently Nana owned the space where her sewing shop used to be."

"Oh, yes. I remember her telling me that she was going to buy that not too long ago. I didn't know what happened to it."

"Well, she bought it and she left it to me, and she wanted me to open the bakery that she always wanted to open."

Perky grinned broadly. "You're going to open a bakery here in Jubilee? Well, we need one of those," she said excitedly.

"So you won't be upset if I open a bakery?"

"Why would I be upset?" Perky asked.

"Well, I mean, you do sell some baked goods here."

"Honey, listen, if I don't have to bake anymore, I'll be delighted. How about I just get stuff from the bakery and sell it here?"

"Oh, that would be fantastic."

"It's time for the new kids to come in here and start running this town. Us older folks would like to rest every now and again you know," Perky said laughing. “Just don’t change things too much. Sometimes the old ways are the best ways.”

"You're not old," Frannie said, squeezing her hand. "Having you and Nana’s other friends in town to help guide me is going to be so helpful. She would've wanted that."

"You're exactly right. We are all here for you, and my best friend Lula would've expected no less from me." It was so rare Frannie heard her grandmother’s real name.

"Perky, do you really think I can do it? I mean, do you really think I can make it a success? I've had so many failures in my life already."

She took both of Frannie’s hands in hers. "I don't *think* you can. I *know* you can. You've got the passion, the talent, and the good heart that's needed to have a very successful bakery here in Jubilee. Everybody will support you, and that's all you need to make any of your dreams come true."

Frannie smiled, determination rising up within her. With Perky and her grandmother's other friends by her side and the rest of the people in town, she knew that she could create the bakery of her dreams and the bakery of her grandmother's dreams. This place was exactly where she was meant to be.

Days had passed, and Madeline was still no closer to figuring out why her mother had actually come to town. But she had to move on with her life and get her work done, including writing her next book and helping Clemmy with the festival. They'd had their first meeting a couple of days ago while Eloise was wandering around the town, taking some time to herself as she put it. Madeline didn't know where she went or what she was up to, but she was glad to have a little bit of free time to herself to unwind and decompress. It didn't last too long. After about an hour, she met up with her mother, had a quick lunch and they went back home. Clemmy had given her some great ideas about what they would do at the festival, and she was just going to try to organize it as best she could.

This morning, she sat at her antique writing desk, her laptop opened to a spreadsheet rather than her current manuscript. She hated spreadsheets. They gave her a headache and made her eyes bleed. Well, maybe not literally, but that's what it felt like. The spreadsheet listed all the tasks, vendors, and the schedule for the festival. Just as she was starting to wrap her mind around how to organize the event, her phone buzzed breaking her concentration. Clemmy's name came up on the screen and she felt a mix of relief and apprehension as she picked up.

"Hey Clemmy. What's going on?"

"Madeline, dear, we've got a little hiccup in the pie contest. Mrs. Thompson isn't going to be able to judge this year. She says her arthritis is acting up again, and she's going to have to go stay with her niece for a while."

Madeline sighed, "Oh, no. I've heard she's really a staple at the festival. I mean, I hope she feels better soon, but now we've got to find a replacement."

"Exactly. Do you have any ideas?"

Madeline was just about to suggest Geneva when her mother walked into the room. She had obviously been eavesdropping on her conversation.

"Why don't you ask that man who won the baking show on TV last year? What is his name? Tim? Tom? I don't know. It was something like that," Eloise interjected.

Madeline looked at her mom. "I'm on a call. Can we talk about this later?" she asked, covering the phone with her hand.

Eloise shrugged. "I was just offering a suggestion. You don't have to get snippy."

Madeline took a deep breath, her patience

wearing thin. She was on a deadline for her new book, and she needed to get to work. Planning the festival was throwing a wrinkle in those plans. "Clemmy, let me think about it and get back to you."

"Sure thing, honey. We've got a little time, but not much."

After she ended the call, Madeline was about to talk to her mother about the unsolicited advice she had given when the doorbell rang. She was grateful for the interruption and opened the door to find Geneva holding a binder and a bag of freshly baked cookies.

"I thought you could use some sugar and some help," Geneva said.

"You're a lifesaver," Madeline responded, opening the door and pointing to the kitchen.

Geneva seemed to sense some tension in the room as she glanced between Madeline and Eloise. "Am I interrupting something?"

"Not at all," Madeline reassured her. "We were just talking about the festival, and my mom had some ideas."

Eloise chimed in. "I was just suggesting that a celebrity judge for the pie contest would draw a bigger crowd."

"That's an interesting idea, but it could overshadow the local talent. I mean, the festival is about community, after all," Geneva said, ever the diplomat.

Eloise frowned, "Well, I think it's a missed opportunity."

Madeline felt the room temperature rise a few degrees. "Mom, this is my project and Clemmy's. I appreciate your input, but I think we've got it under control."

Eloise's eyes narrowed, but she didn't say anything. Geneva took that moment to pull Madeline aside.

"Hey, are you okay? You seem a little frazzled today."

Madeline sighed, "I'm just overwhelmed. The festival's a big deal and having my mom here is a bit complicated. Plus, I'm working on my book."

Geneva squeezed her hand. "You're doing a great job. And as for your mom, just give it time. Relationships like this don't mend overnight."

Just then, Madeline's phone buzzed again. It was from Clemmy. *"Good news. The local high school band is confirmed for the festival. They're preparing a special fall medley."*

Madeline's spirits lifted instantly. "Hey, great news. The high school band is in," she told Geneva.

"That's wonderful."

"Listen, do you think you can step in for Mrs. Thompson and be our judge for the pie contest?"

Geneva smiled. "Eat a bunch of pies and give my opinion? I suppose you could twist my arm."

Madeline hugged her. "Thank you!"

CHAPTER 4

Frannie sat on a folding chair in the middle of the vacant space that was going to become her dream bakery. The walls were completely bare, and the floors were a little scuffed up, but in her mind she saw beautiful pastel colored walls, rustic wooden tables, and the warm glow of a chandelier hanging overhead. She thought about the countertop that would be filled with freshly baked pastries, and the air that would be tinged with the scent of cinnamon and vanilla. Her phone buzzed yet again, pulling her out of her daydream. It was another email from a contractor with a quote.

Her heart sank for the third time today. It was way over her budget. She looked around her empty space, feeling like her dream was suddenly as hollow as the room. How was she going to do this? She couldn't afford to spend a lot of money to renovate the space. Sure, it was usable, but she had to get special ovens, a cash register, a display case, tables, chairs. There was so much to think about, not to mention utilities. It was all overwhelming. Her grandmother had left her the house and the space, but she didn't have much money to speak of, and Frannie was starting to wonder whether this was a possibility at all. Maybe she'd had her head too much in the clouds. Maybe she had gotten excited for nothing and would have to sell the space and the house and go back home, feeling like a failure yet again.

Just then the door creaked open slightly, and a man stepped inside. It took her a moment to recognize him, but when she did, her heart sped up. It was Cole, her high school sweetheart, standing there as if the years had all folded in on themselves. She hadn't seen him since just after high school, and she honestly didn't think she would ever see him again. Although Frannie had come to town mostly in the summers and on holidays, she had lived with her grandmother for some of her high school years after having a falling out with her parents. Teenagers were tough, and Frannie was no exception. Her grandmother had welcomed her with open arms, and she had attended Jubilee High School for over two years.

During that time, she had fallen in love with Cole - a tall, dark, and handsome guy that every girl in school was obsessed with, and for some reason he had fallen for her. But when it had ended, it had broken her heart, and she wasn't sure if she ever wanted to see him again. Now in her thirties, she felt foolish about that, but looking at him, she definitely knew there were still some feelings there, deep down.

"Cole, is that you?" she stammered.

"In the flesh," he said, his eyes meeting hers. "I heard you were back in town to take care of your grandmother's house, but I had no idea you were opening a bakery." She felt a rush of emotions - joy, surprise, and a twinge of sadness. There was just something deep down in her heart that made her sad when she thought about the fact that she hadn't married him after high school.

"What are you doing here?"

"I moved back to take care of my dad. He's not doing so well. I started my own contracting business here. Actually, I took over my dad's."

"Oh, Cole, I'm so sorry to hear about your dad, but it's good you're back. Jubilee missed you, I'm sure." He looked around the vacant space, his eyes narrowing as if he was calculating costs.

"Looks like you could use some help here."

"That is an understatement," she said gesturing around the empty room, "The quotes I'm getting are sky high. I'm already going to have to take out a small business loan just to get the equipment here." He scratched his chin, pondering.

"Can I see the quotes?"

"Sure," Frannie said, handing him her phone. He looked at each one carefully.

"What if I told you I could do it for a lot less? I want to help you out, Frannie, and I'm trying to build my business. Maybe you can give me a good recommendation?" Her heart fluttered at his words, but a part of her wondered why he was offering this. Was it just business, or was there something else?

"Why would you do that?" He looked away for a moment as if he was gathering his thoughts.

"Let's just say for old time's sake. And it's high time this town had a good bakery."

"Okay," Frannie said, feeling both excited and nervous. "Let's do it." They shook hands, and the touch lingered for a moment longer than it probably should have. It was like they were feeling many years worth of unsaid words and missed opportunities.

"I'll write up some ideas and get started as soon as you give me the green light," he said, finally, breaking the silence.

"You have yourself a deal." Cole nodded and made his way to the door. As he stepped out, he looked back and their eyes met one more time.

"I'll see you soon, Frannie."

"See you soon," she said. As the door closed behind him, she felt a whirlwind of thoughts and feelings. The vacant space around her suddenly seemed full of possibilities, as if his presence had breathed new life into her dreams. But, it wasn't just the bakery that seemed within reach now. It was a second chance at something she thought she'd lost forever.

She picked up her phone and deleted the other emails from contractors. She'd made her choice. Cole was going to help her fix up this bakery. It would be a future filled with fresh starts and the sweet taste of what might be.

Madeline sat in her cozy living room overlooking the mountains, sipping on a cup of chamomile tea, trying to calm her frazzled nerves. Ever since her mother had arrived, she'd been on edge. It was like walking on eggshells. It had only been a little over a week, but it was very difficult to get much done with her around. She was constantly looking over her shoulder, wondering if her mother's critical nature was going to come out.

She heard the rustling of paper coming from the guest room. Her curiosity got the best of her, so she set her cup on the coffee table and walked down the hallway. The door to the guest room was slightly open, and through the gap, she could see her mother sitting on the bed, surrounded by old family photos. Madeline kept them in a box in the top of the closet of that room. Until now, she'd forgotten about it.

For a minute, Madeline hesitated, her hand hovering over the doorknob. Her relationship with her mother had been complicated for most of her life. There was a tangle of emotions swirling in her that she couldn't quite unravel, and she wondered if she would ever be able to. But something about the sight of seeing her mother looking at the old photos, nudged her to push the door open.

"Hey, Mom. What are you doing?" Madeline asked, her voice softer than she had intended.

Eloise looked up, startled.

"Oh, I didn't know you were standing there. I was

just looking at some of these old photos, reminiscing. Your father loved taking pictures, you know." Madeline was surprised to hear her mention her ex-husband without a sneer on her face. Their divorce had been beyond ugly, which was probably warranted given her father's infidelity.

Madeline felt her guard drop slightly. Her father had been the glue that had held their family together, but when he left, she and her mother had drifted even further apart. Madeline hadn't heard from him since she was in high school.

"Yes, he did."

Eloise picked up a photograph of a younger version of themselves. They were at a family picnic, all sunshine and smiles.

"In the end, all we have are the memories. Things don't always turn out how we'd planned, even with our best intentions. Sometimes the family we thought we'd build isn't what we end up with."

Madeline sat down beside her mother, taking the photo from her hand and looking at it. She remembered that day. The smell of the freshly cut grass in the park. The laughter. The feeling that everything was right in the world.

"I sure do miss those times," Madeline said. She felt sad and a little guilty that her mother had commented on not having family around. Madeline knew exactly what that meant, but she didn't know why she should feel so much turmoil over it. Surely her mother realized that the reason Madeline wasn't around was because of how she was treated. Eloise nodded, her eyes slightly misty,

"So do I, Madeline. So do I." For a moment, they just sat there quietly, each of them lost in their own thoughts. There was a shared past between them and so many unspoken feelings. It was a touching moment to Madeline, a fragile truce in their ongoing emotional war. Then Eloise broke the silence.

"You know, after your daddy left, that house felt so empty. I would just sit in his office for hours looking at his books, his papers, trying to understand what I did wrong that made him leave us."

Madeline had been wrapped up in her own grief about losing her relationship with her father, and now she felt a pang of guilt. She'd forgotten that her mother was grieving at the time, too.

"I'm sorry, Mom. I should have been there for you more over the years." Eloise looked at her.

"We all cope in our own ways, but you know it's never too late for us to make amends."

Madeline felt her heart swell with a mixture of hope and yet apprehension.

"So, is that why you're here, Mom? You want to make amends and repair our relationship. Is that really it?"

Eloise hesitated. Her eyes darting away.

"Let's just say I'm here because it's time."

It was a non-answer, and Madeline felt frustrated. She swallowed it down, deciding to let it go for the moment.

"Well, I'm glad you're here. It's a start." Eloise set the photos back in the box and looked around the room.

"You've made a nice home for yourself, Madeline. Even if I don't understand it."

Madeline's eyes widened. That was surprising given all the comments her mother had made when she arrived just a few days ago. Compliments from her mother were as rare as snow in July. She didn't know quite what to say.

"Thank you. That means a lot to me."

Just then, Madeline's phone buzzed on the nightstand. She glanced at the screen. It was an unknown number. For a moment she was going to answer it, but something stopped her. Instead, she silenced her phone. Eloise stood up, stretching out her arms.

"You know, it's getting late. I think I'll turn in for the night."

Madeline nodded, her mind a whirlpool of conflicting emotions.

"Goodnight, Mom."

Madeline walked out of the room and shut the door behind her. She dialed her most familiar phone number.

"Hey, it's me," she said when Brady picked up.

"Hey. How are you? How is everything going with your mom?" Brady's voice was always warm. It was a comforting balm to her frazzled nerves. She sighed, sinking back into the chair in the living room.

"It's complicated, Brady. You know how it is with family. We had a moment, a real moment, but then she put up a wall again. I don't know if I'll ever be able to get through to her."

Brady was quiet for a minute as if he was choosing his words carefully.

"Maybe it's not about getting through to her, Madeline. Maybe it's about letting her come to you in her own time, in her own way. It might not be the way that you expect or the way that you want. I've had this situation with my own sister. You know that. You can't control how another person responds, but you can give them grace."

"And what if it never happens, Brady? What then?"

He sighed, his voice tinged with sadness.

"Well, then at least you know you tried, and sometimes that is all we can do."

They talked for a few more minutes, and as she hung up the phone, Madeline felt reassured, but still uncertain. She walked upstairs and laid on her bed, staring at the ceiling, her mind racing with thoughts she couldn't quite silence. As she drifted off to sleep, she just couldn't shake the feeling that she was standing at the edge of something vast and unknown. She stepped into the void as she closed her eyes, knowing that whatever lay on the other side would at least bring her answers, and hopefully closure, to so many things in her life.

Frannie sat at a small, weathered wooden table in the corner of Perky's Coffee Shop. Her fingers were wrapped around a now cold café au lait. She noticed the vintage floral wallpaper that had seen better days but had been there since she was a kid. As she waited, she swore that her heart rate sped up every time she heard the front door ding. Her eyes flitted nervously between her almost empty cup and the door. There was an antique clock on the wall ticking away.

As the door finally creaked open, a familiar sound cut through the hum of conversations and clinking coffee cups, Frannie looked up to meet Cole's eyes as he stepped inside. He was dressed in his normal rugged, yet stylish, manner: a plaid shirt, well-worn blue jeans and work boots. His attire spoke of a man who could swing a hammer just as easily as he could navigate a spreadsheet. He smiled at her, and her heart didn't just skip a beat. It felt like it stopped altogether for a moment.

"Hey, Frannie," he said, his voice filled with a warmth that seemed to reach across the room. "Sorry I'm a little late. There was a last-minute issue at a job site."

She felt tense muscles finally relax. "No problem. I've been enjoying my coffee, or at least I was," she said, laughing.

Cole ordered a black coffee from the counter and then sat down across from her. "You still love a good café au lait, I see."

"Some things never change," she said, her eyes meeting his. She had forgotten just how blue his eyes were, like two pools of ocean water, and his hair was as black as midnight. Cole always got a great tan in the summer, and she could see that he was keeping that up by doing a lot of work outdoors.

He set a thick folder down next to his steaming cup of coffee that the server slid in front of him. "Ready to get down to business and talk about your bakery?"

She nodded, her eyes looking down at the folder. "I'm all ears. What do you have for me?"

He opened the folder with a sense of ceremony, revealing meticulously organized drawings, sketches, and spreadsheets. "So, I've crunched the numbers, and I think we can make this work within your budget. We're going to have to be strategic, but it's doable."

She leaned in, her eyes wide, as she tried to take in the numbers. She had never been much of a numbers person, but she could gather what he was talking about. Everything looked reasonable.

"This is incredible, Cole. How did you manage to get the cost down this low?"

He looked up, locking eyes with her. "Let's just say I have some good contacts in the industry, and I'm willing to put in some extra hours myself. But more than that, I believe in this, Frannie. I believe in you."

The words hung in the air between them for a

moment, charged with some kind of emotion that Frannie couldn't put her finger on. A warmth spread from her chest to the tip of her fingers settling in her very core. Sitting with Cole, it felt like no time had passed at all.

"Thank you, Cole. You have no idea how much this means to me. I can't wait to open the bakery to honor my grandmother's memory."

For a moment, their eyes met, and held and then Frannie felt a door crack open, a door to questions long buried and the words left unsaid. She saw it in his eyes, too. There was a hesitance as if he was standing on the edge of a confession. But then as quickly as it had appeared, the moment vanished. He looked away.

"So," he said, clearing his throat as he shuffled the papers, "we'll just start with the basics. Flooring, walls. We'll move on to more specialized stuff like the ovens and display cases. I've also factored in the electrical work for that chandelier you mentioned. You can see that number here."

Frannie nodded, grateful that they had changed topics, even though a part of her ached to know what he wanted to say. There were so many unanswered questions about their breakup all those years ago, so many things she wanted to ask, but the answers didn't matter now.

"Sounds like a plan. So when can we get started?"

"My crew can start as early as next week."

"Next week?" Frannie's heart was soaring. "That is beyond fantastic."

He closed the folder, his hands lingering on the cover as if sealing a pact. "The sooner we start, the sooner you can open those doors and fill Jubilee with the smell of fresh-baked pound cakes and cinnamon streusel."

"I can't wait for that day."

He reached across the table, his fingers lightly brushing against hers. "Frannie, about what happened in the past..."

Just then, Perky ran over, her eyes twinkling. "I couldn't help but overhear. Cole, you're a godsend. You're going to help Frannie get the bakery open?" The moment shattered like a delicate ornament on a hardwood floor. He pulled his hand back, and Frannie felt a sense of loss that she wasn't expecting.

"Well, I haven't done anything yet," Cole said, laughing. "But I'm committed to making this happen."

Perky winked at Frannie. "And we're all behind

you, darling. This town needs a bakery, and who better than our own Frannie Franklin?"

"I'll do my best not to let anyone down," she said, feeling the weight of responsibility on her shoulders.

"You won't let anyone down," Cole said, his voice low, almost intimate. "I know you won't."

As he gathered his papers and stood up, Frannie felt a whirlwind of emotions: relief, excitement, concern. She said goodbye and watched him walk out the door, thinking about building that dream bakery together and maybe getting to explore some past events that never had closure.

CHAPTER 5

Madeline felt a mix of excitement and worry as she and her mother got into the golf cart that would take them down the road to Brady's farm. They were going to have dinner and carve pumpkins with Anna in anticipation of Halloween.

The sun was just setting, casting a warm glow over the fall leaves. The air was crisp, but it wasn't yet too cold. It was the perfect evening to have a cozy dinner with Brady, Jasmine, and Anna.

"Are you sure this contraption is safe?" Eloise asked, looking around the golf cart skeptically. Madeline laughed. "It's just a short ride, Mom. I'm sure you'll be fine. I don't have any plans to kill us both."

As they pulled up at Brady's property, Madeline noticed her mother's eyes get bigger at the sight of the trailer where Brady, Jasmine, and Anna were currently living. The house was still under construction after Brady's family home burned down a few months before. The new house stood like a skeletal promise in the barn's background.

"This is where he lives?" Eloise asked, criticism dripping from her voice. "It looks awfully small for three people."

"I told you they're staying here while the house is being rebuilt." Madeline had already told her that, but she just had to say something when they pulled up. Not that there was anything wrong with someone living in a trailer as long as they were happy and had what they needed. She chose to ignore her mother's judgment because she was excited about having a nice evening with her boyfriend and his family.

Brady came out to greet them, a smile lighting up his face when he saw Madeline. He hugged her tightly and then quickly pecked her on the lips before looking at Eloise. "Hello, again. It's great to see you."

"The pleasure is mine," Eloise replied. Her tone

was polite, but reserved. They walked toward the trailer and Brady led them past a small pen.

"Would you like to meet Gilbert?" he asked with a playful grin on his face. Madeline shook her head and looked at him with a warning.

"Gilbert?" Eloise asked, raising an eyebrow.

"He's my crazy rescue goat. He's quite the character, as Madeline can tell you," Brady explained. It seemed that curiosity got the better of Eloise, so she agreed to go over and meet the wild little goat. The moment they walked into his pen, crazy Gilbert lived up to his name, prancing around and letting out a series of bleats that sounded like he was laughing at them. Despite herself, Eloise actually chuckled. Madeline saw her mother's eyes soften for a moment. It was something she hadn't seen in quite some time.

"Well, I guess you could say he is unique," Eloise said, carefully reaching out and petting the top of Gilbert's head.

"Unique would be one way to put it," Brady said laughing.

Once they walked inside the trailer, the aroma of vegetable soup and fresh baked cornbread filled the air. Jasmine was in the kitchen putting the finishing touches on a big pitcher of sweet tea, while Anna sat on the couch, her eyes glued to something on the television.

"Anna, look who's here," Jasmine called to her daughter. Anna looked up, her face lighting up. "Aunt Madeline!"

Eloise looked over at her daughter and whispered, "Aunt Madeline?"

"We're a family here, Mom. I know you don't understand that, but try not to be too judgy about it, okay?" Madeline bent down and gave Anna a hug. "How are you, sweetie?"

"I'm good. Are we still carving pumpkins tonight?"

"You bet," Madeline said smiling.

After a little more small talk, they sat down at the dinner table. The trailer wasn't a big place, and the table barely fit all of them, so it was a cozy affair. As usual, there was tension simmering just below the surface. Eloise asked questions that bordered on intrusive, like how much longer the house was going to take to complete and whether Jasmine had a job. Madeline kept feeling herself cringe, but was grateful for Brady's grace in navigating the conversation.

"Mom, I told you Jasmine is my assistant," Madeline interjected. She hoped to steer the conversation away from any sensitive topics like Jasmine's past or why they were living with Brady. Thankfully, her mother didn't seem to notice that it was odd in any way.

"Jasmine has been a huge help in my business and with organizing the upcoming harvest festival."

"Oh, yes, the harvest festival," Eloise said, "That seems to be quite the exciting event around here."

"It is," Madeline said. "And it's a lot of work. Like I said, Jasmine has been invaluable to me in so many ways."

Brady walked over and brought the pot of vegetable soup, steam rising through the air. Jasmine had already placed the cornbread on the table, along with a small plate with a stick of butter. Madeline loved the comforting scent of the foods. Brady placed an empty bowl in front of Eloise and handed her the ladle. "Guests first."

"Thank you, Brady. I'm sure it'll be wonderful." She reached over and scooped out two ladles full of vegetable soup and then took a piece of cornbread from the plate. After taking her first bite, she smiled slightly. "This is actually quite good."

"Thank you. It's an old family recipe," Brady said.

As they moved on to everyone eating the meal, Anna decided it was her turn to chat with Madeline's mother. "Do you like to carve pumpkins, Grandma Eloise?"

Eloise stared at Anna like she didn't know how to respond. "Well, it's been many years, but I think I could probably give it a try."

Madeline was shocked that her mother didn't correct Anna and say not to call her grandma. No one had ever called her grandma. Being an only child, Madeline was Eloise's only chance at having grandchildren. Although she'd never mentioned it over the years, Madeline had wondered if that was part of the reason her mother seemed so resentful of her. There was nothing she could do about it now.

Anna beamed. "I'm so excited. It's my first time carving a pumpkin so we can learn together."

Eloise shot a glance at Madeline who was sitting next to her. Madeline leaned in to whisper to her mother. "Jasmine and Anna left a very difficult situation a few months ago. They're still finding their footing, so there are a lot of firsts for Anna."

Eloise looked at her daughter, her eyes searching. "I see," she finally said in a soft voice.

After dinner, it was time for pumpkin carving. Brady had set up a picnic table outside next to a light pole he had near the barn. Anna's eyes widened at the sight of two pumpkins and all the carving tools.

"Can I do that one?" She pointed at the most particularly plump pumpkin.

"Of course you can," Brady said, lifting it up onto the table. Madeline admired him from afar, his muscular arms seeming to have no trouble picking up the pumpkin. He was the most handsome man she'd ever seen in person, and she was so thankful he was hers.

They started the carving with Eloise sitting next to Anna consulting on what they should do. "Don't you think we should do a scary face?" Eloise suggested.

Anna crinkled her nose and shook her head. "I don't like scary pumpkins. I think we should do a funny face."

The two of them sat there together, and Madeline marveled at how her mother seemed to settle right into being a grandmother figure. She wished it could be this way forever, but she knew that eventually her mother was going to do or say something to complicate the situation. Plus, she wasn't staying long. That much Madeline was sure of. Her mother loved living in the suburbs and spending time with her friends at the senior center. She lived in an over fifty-five community, and she had never been one who was great with children. Maybe that was one of the reasons Madeline had never had any of her own, or maybe it was just that she ran out of time and never found the right man. Now that she had the right man, she didn't have the right body for it.

"This isn't that hard at all," Anna said smiling as she looked over at Madeline.

"Well, you're doing a great job. So are you, Mom." Eloise shot her a look and rolled her eyes. But Madeline was actually giving her a real compliment. She was doing a great job at fitting in and being kind. Madeline started to unclench her shoulder muscles as Brady walked over and put his arm around her.

"This is going well," he said softly.

"Yeah, a lot better than I thought it was going to go."

"Do you guys need anything else? I was going to start cleaning up the kitchen." Jasmine asked.

"Let me help you with that," Madeline said.

"No, no. Stay out here and enjoy the pumpkin carving." She walked into the trailer, and Madeline turned her attention back to Anna and Eloise.

"Look, Grandma Eloise. I got his tooth right," Anna said giggling as she gave the pumpkin a one tooth smile.

Eloise smiled. "That's wonderful, Anna."

When they finished, they placed candles in the carved pumpkins and lit them. The flickering glow seeming to cast a spell over the farm. Even Eloise eventually seemed to relax. Her eyes meeting Madeline in a moment of unspoken understanding.

When it was time to say goodbye, Anna had already tuckered out and was asleep on the sofa. Eloise looked at Brady. "Thank you for dinner. The soup was delicious and the cornbread, too."

"You can thank Jasmine for that," Brady said, pointing at his sister standing in the kitchen. She waved her hand and laughed.

"Well, it was wonderful. Thank you for inviting me. I hope we can do it again."

As they climbed back into the golf cart, Madeline felt such a sense of relief wash over her. There were awkward moments during the evening, as usual, but for the first time she felt like maybe she might get her mother to understand why she was charmed by Jubilee.

"So, did you have a good time?" Madeline asked her mom as they drove back up the hill to her house. Eloise paused for a moment.

"You know what? I believe I did."

Madeline smiled as they pulled the golf cart into

the driveway. Maybe it wouldn't be such a bad holiday season after all.

Frannie sat at her Nana's kitchen table, cell phone in her hand, and her heart pounding in her chest. She had been sitting there staring at her phone for what seemed like hours, her thumb hovering over the phone number to her supervisor at the hospital.

She knew this was going to sound like the world's craziest call. Karen, her supervisor, had become a great friend over the years. Frannie was also a very good nurse. It was something she had wanted to do since she was a little kid, but now she was going to call her friend and tell her that she quit, that she was moving back to her grandmother's tiny town and running a bakery. It seemed insane when she thought about it, giving up her cushy salary, her nice apartment in the city, and her health benefits. Instead, she was going to become one of the thousands of entrepreneurs who tried to open a business every year, most of them failing miserably before it was over.

Maybe she was crazy. Maybe this was something

she shouldn't do, but she just felt so pulled by her grandmother's words and the way that she had confidence in Frannie.

Finally, she pressed the button and took a deep breath. The phone rang twice before Karen picked up.

"Frannie, how are you? We've missed you at the hospital. It's just not the same here without you."

"Hey, Karen. I've missed everybody too, but I'm calling because I need to talk to you about something important, and I just need to get it out."

"Of course. What's going on?"

Frannie took another deep breath. "I've made a decision. You're going to think I've lost my mind, but I'm not coming back to the hospital."

"What? But, Frannie, you're one of our best nurses. You've been here for almost six years now."

"I know. I hope you can understand."

"Are you going to another hospital? Or are you going to work at that doctor's office that keeps trying to pull you away from us?"

Frannie laughed. "No. I'm going to open a bakery in Jubilee, Georgia, in honor of my Nana."

There was a long pause on the other end of the line. "Wow, Frannie, that's really a big step. You're going to give up your nursing career to run a bakery? Do you think that's a great idea? Are you sure?"

"Yes, I'm sure. It's something I've always wanted to do, something I shared with my grandmother a lot, and now it just feels like the right time."

"Well, we will all be sad to lose you, but you know I wish you all the best. I'm sure you will make your nana proud."

"Thank you, Karen. It really means a lot."

"And, hey, if you ever change your mind and want to come back, you know you always have a place here with us."

After hanging up, Frannie felt relieved, but a huge weight on her shoulders at the same time. Now, it was real. It wasn't just some idea in her head. It was an actual real thing that was going to happen. She had done it. She had quit her job. She had ended her nursing career and taken the first step toward making her dream a reality, and now the real work would begin.

Just as she was getting over the phone call, there was a knock at the door that startled her. She got up and walked over to see Geneva standing there holding a casserole dish covered with foil.

"Hey, Geneva. I'm so glad to see you. I've been meaning to drop by, but I've just been so busy trying to get this place cleaned up and work on opening the bakery."

"Yes, I heard about the bakery. I thought maybe you could use some company, and maybe a home cooked meal."

"That sounds wonderful. Come in. I could really use somebody to talk to right now."

Frannie went to the kitchen and got some plates and silverware before walking out onto the back porch where Geneva sat at the table overlooking the rolling hills behind her grandmother's house. Geneva uncovered the dish to reveal mashed potatoes, green beans, and fried chicken. The aroma filled the air. It was comforting and familiar to Frannie.

As they started to eat, Frannie felt a sense of peace wash over her. She loved Geneva. Geneva had been around just as much as Perky and Clemmy when she was little. These were her grandmother's best friends, and even though she would much rather have her grandmother there right now, they were wonderful stand-ins.

"So, I just called the hospital where I work," Frannie said, taking a bite of her mashed potatoes. "I told them I'm not coming back, that I'm going to open a bakery here in Jubilee. I think they're probably assuming I've lost my mind."

Geneva laughed. "Oh, Frannie, your grandmother would be so tickled for you. She was very proud that you were a nurse. It's a noble profession. But, she talked to me many times about how she wished that the two of you could open a bakery together. It was one of her big life dreams."

Frannie felt sad. "I wish I had done it sooner. I didn't know it meant so much to her until I read her letter. If I had known..."

Geneva held up her hand, "No regrets, dear. Regrets get you nowhere. They keep you stuck. This is what was supposed to happen. This is *how* it was supposed to happen. And even though I know you miss your grandmother, she is right here with you. She is looking down at you right now, clapping her hands and shouting for joy that you're finally going to live out both of your dreams."

"I hope so. I miss her so much, Geneva. She was always there for me even when I didn't come around as often as I should. Now that she's gone, I feel like I'm navigating through life without my compass."

Geneva reached across the table and took her hand. "I knew Lula since we were kids in school. She was my oldest friend. I miss her every day, but let me tell you something, she's always going to be with you, Frannie. She's there in the way that you laugh, the way that you care for people, and she will be in every cupcake you bake."

Frannie's eyes widened as she looked at her. "She said something similar in her letter to me."

Geneva chuckled. "That doesn't surprise me. We were a lot alike."

"Thank you for bringing the food, Geneva, but more than that, thank you for bringing the company. It means the world to me."

They ate in silence for a few moments, each of them lost in their own thoughts as the sun set, casting a glow over the hills. "Lula used to say that the secret to a good life is doing what you love with the people you love, and I can't think of a better way for you to honor her memory than opening that bakery and doing what you love for the people of this town that she loved so much."

"I've had my doubts wondering if I'm doing the right thing, but I feel like Nana is speaking through you and telling me that I'm on the right path."

"She's always with you, guiding you, and she always will be."

As they finished their meal and chatted about other things going on in town, including the upcoming harvest festival, Frannie felt at home for the first time in a long time. Not that she didn't love her friends back at the hospital, but she never felt like she was quite in the right place. She always felt like she was a puzzle piece that didn't quite fit. But, in this moment, at this time, sitting on her grand-mother's porch overlooking those frolicking hills, she finally felt like the pieces all fit.

CHAPTER 6

Madeline pushed open the door to Away With Words, Clemmy's quaint little bookstore that had been a staple in Jubilee for years. She allowed her mother to walk through first and then followed. The familiar scent of paper and coffee filled the air. It was an instant comfort for Madeline. Of course, being an author, she loved the smell of both things.

Eloise scanned the room with a mixture of curiosity and skepticism as she did most of the time.

"Madeline, it's great to see you," Clemmy said, as she came out from behind the counter. Clemmy had a sense of style unlike any other. She had short gray hair and wore cat-eye glasses and a full face of makeup. Madeline hoped to be as beautiful as her in ten years when she was in her mid-sixties. Clemmy looked like she had always been a very stylish woman.

"And you must be Eloise. I've heard so much about you," Clemmy said, extending her hand.

"Clementine, is it? What an interesting little shop you have here," Eloise said.

Clemmy laughed. "Yes, my full name is Clementine but everybody calls me Clemmy. You can, too." Madeline wanted to laugh because it was obvious that Clemmy wasn't going to be intimidated by Eloise. "We like to think of this as a sanctuary for anyone who loves books."

"Well, I suppose that's a good thing then," Eloise said.

"I'm just going to show Mom around, and then you and I can chat for a moment about the final touches for the harvest festival."

"Sounds like a plan," Clemmy said, turning to walk back over to the cash register to check out a customer.

Madeline led her mother through the maze of bookshelves, her fingers lightly grazing the spines of some of the novels that she wanted to pick up.

"Mom, this is where my books are displayed. Right here in the romance section," Madeline said proudly, smiling as she pointed.

Eloise looked over at the shelf, her eyes narrowing as she read the titles, “Love Under The Harvest Moon, A Christmas Love Story…” She started naming off titles and scrunching her nose like she smelled something bad. "I guess they're very quaint. Which ones are yours?"

Madeline pointed at hers, which were on one of the upper shelves. "Clemmy keeps stock of these three books most of the time. Those are my best-sellers."

"You mean from years ago?" Eloise said. "Didn't you tell me that your books had stopped selling recently?"

"Well, they don't sell as well as they used to. People like small-town books, and that's what I'm working on now."

"Oh, Madeline, this is a cute little town and everything, but I can't believe you picked up your whole life to live here just because your books weren't selling. I still think you should check into another career path."

"Mom, what did I tell you? This conversation is off-limits. I love it here in Jubilee, and I'm not leaving."

Eloise picked up a copy of one of the romance books, but not Madeline's. "Well, if writing about small-town love affairs and holiday miracles is something that keeps you entertained, I guess who am I to judge?"

Madeline clenched her jaw. "It's not just about entertaining me, Mom. People love my books. I want to create something meaningful, something that brings people joy and helps them through their toughest situations."

Before Eloise could say anything else Clemmy walked over, almost looking like she sensed that Madeline needed to be rescued.

"Care for some coffee?" She held out a little silver tray with two cups of coffee on it, each with a bit of whipped cream on the top. "I thought you ladies might enjoy something hot since it's getting cooler outside."

"Oh, how delightful," Eloise said, taking one of the coffees. "Although this will probably ruin my dinner."

"I'm sure it will be fine, Mom," Madeline said, rolling her eyes at Clemmy. "Thank you for the coffee."

"You're welcome. You know we always like to make our customers feel comfortable."

Madeline shot Clemmy a grateful look as she led her mother to a different part of the store. Eloise liked to read, somewhat at least, so she took her to the mystery section and told her to pick something out. Secretly Madeline hoped it would keep her occupied at home in those moments where Madeline just needed a minute to herself.

"Why don't you look around over here, Mom? I'm going to go chat with Clemmy for just a moment."

"Okay. I mean, there's not much of a selection, so I don't think it will take me long," Eloise said.

"Got it," Madeline called back as she walked over to Clemmy.

"How are you doing?" Clemmy asked, as they got around the corner.

"Is it possible that I could just leave her here with you?" Madeline asked.

Clemmy laughed. "So it's been that challenging?"

"It's been more challenging than I ever could have imagined."

"I'm so sorry, Madeline. How long is she staying?"

"I have no idea. She doesn't seem to be making any moves to leave. It's like she just showed up at my house and has moved in with me."

"Well, it is your mother, and I know you feel a responsibility to her, but why don't you just ask?"

"I don't know. I just still get this feeling that she's here for some reason and she's not telling me yet. I just keep waiting for some big reveal to happen."

Clemmy reached out and squeezed Madeline's arm. "Is there anything I can do?"

"No. And honestly, I'm thankful for the harvest festival. It's giving me a reason to be distracted by something."

"Speaking of that, do we want to talk about the apple cider cart?"

"I think that we have Ethan working on that?"

"Oh yes. I think he agreed to man that station for us. That's right. I think most everything is tied up then. We just need to have the fall festival and enjoy ourselves."

Madeline laughed. "I don't think I'm going to enjoy myself. I think I'm going to be a nervous wreck running around trying to make sure everything's going well."

Clemmy laughed. "Remember, it's supposed to be a fun time."

"Yeah, I'll try to remember that."

Clemmy and Madeline walked back toward Eloise, who was standing in the middle of the store like she had never been in a bookstore before and didn't know what to do.

"Are you finding anything?" Clemmy asked.

"I found this one. I suppose it looks okay." She held up a random mystery book. "I see this section over here labeled self-help. I guess that's the refuge of the lost and confused. Do you sell many of these, Clementine?"

Clemmy smiled, having the patience of Job. "Actually, yes, I do. It seems like people find what they need among these shelves, whether it's fiction or nonfiction."

Eloise chuckled under her breath. "Well, I suppose in a small town like this, there's not much else you can do but read and think about your problems."

Madeline felt her cheeks turn red. "Mom, that's not fair. Jubilee has a lot to offer and so does this bookstore."

Eloise sighed. "I didn't mean to offend, dear. I'm just trying to understand why you love this place so much. It's just not like you."

Madeline took in a deep breath and chose her words as carefully as possible. "This town, this bookstore, they're a part of who I am. And now the new stories that I write are inspired by the community and the love that I have found here, and I really wish you could see that."

Clemmy backed away before Madeline realized

it. She was probably feeling quite uncomfortable at the interaction they were having. Madeline was embarrassed.

They made their way up to the counter, and Madeline felt frustration at the fact that her mother may never understand her love for Jubilee or her love for writing. She thought it might be time to put up boundaries again.

Clemmy rang up their purchase, her eyes meeting Madeline's. "Come back anytime, Eloise. You know there's always a story waiting for you here."

"Thank you, Clementine," Eloise said, sounding snobby.

Madeline said goodbye to Clemmy and then they stepped back out into the crisp fall air. She realized that her relationship with her mother was a work in progress. It was like a story unfolding before her. The only problem was she didn't seem to have any control of the ending.

Madeline was feeling a whirlwind of emotions as she stepped onto the sidewalk in the downtown square. Today was Jubilee's

Harvest Festival. It would be her first one and definitely the first one that she had ever planned in her life. She didn't consider herself to be the most organized person, even though people assumed that she was because she was an author.

Her hiking boots crunched against the fallen autumn leaves, and the air was tinged with a wonderful blend of cinnamon, nutmeg and the earthy scent of pumpkins and hay. She could hear the laughter of children filling the air, and it was mixed with the melodies of a local folk music band that was playing guitars and banjos standing under the gazebo.

She stood for a moment and took in a deep breath, savoring the moment, looking at her and Clemmy's vision come to life. The tapestry of their community made her feel proud, but she didn't have time to stand around. There were a lot of things to do, including checking on all the different stations they had set up and making sure things were going to go as planned.

Her first stop was at the raffle ticket table where Geneva and her mother were sitting. They sat behind a makeshift desk, which was made of hay bales and a long wooden plank. There were stacks of raffle tickets, a cash box, and a glass jar filled with names that were neatly arranged. Eloise looked up when Madeline approached, her eyes scanning the festival behind her daughter.

"It's all so very quaint and rustic," Eloise said, her tone a mix of curiosity and skepticism.

Geneva laughed. "Well, we've sold a good bunch of tickets, Madeline. The high school football team will have new uniforms in no time."

Madeline felt proud of that. "That's great. I'm sure you two are doing an amazing job."

Eloise picked up one of the tickets, looking at it closely. "So, with these tickets we're selling, do they actually win something good?"

Geneva giggled. "Well, the grand prize is a weekend getaway at the inn. I'd say that's pretty worthwhile."

"You mean the inn right over there?" Eloise asked, pointing. "How is that exciting?"

"Mom, quit saying things like that. People in this town really love that inn, and it's a great place to get away for a weekend."

"I wasn't being critical. Just asking a question," Eloise said, going back to looking down at the tickets.

"Well, I'd better keep moving. There's a lot of stuff for me to check on," Madeline said. Before she walked away, her phone buzzed with a text from Brady.

Gilbert is a superstar. Come see.

Madeline waved at her mother and Geneva before trotting off to the petting zoo where Brady had several of his animals in a large pen. Little children were walking around, petting and feeding them. All of them were enamored by Gilbert, the goat who was happily munching on some hay.

"Hey, you," Brady said, his eyes lighting up as Madeline approached. "I have to say that Gilbert's drawing quite the crowd."

Madeline laughed. "As he always does. We both know he's a natural star. He really should move to Hollywood."

"And don't forget, I've got tractor duty for the hayride later."

"I would never forget," Madeline said. "But, I do have to run. There is so much for me to check on to make sure all of this is going to go off without a hitch."

"Of course. I'll see you later," Brady said, giving her a quick kiss on the cheek.

The next place Madeline went was over to the cakewalk game. Heather and Lanelle, the mother and daughter duo that ran the local inn, were directing a group of eager participants who were trying to win each of the cakes that had been made by some of the best bakers in town. The circle of numbered squares was filled with people stepping in time to the music, their eyes on the prize: the next delicious homemade cake.

"Heather, Lanelle, how are we doing over here?" Madeline asked, her eyes scanning the area.

Heather smiled. "Madeline, it's a hit. We've already gone through three cakes, and the fourth is about to be won."

"And we've got a red velvet and carrot cake still to go," Lanelle chimed in.

Madeline felt her spirits lift even higher. "You two are doing great. Keep the fun going."

She turned to leave and spotted Ethan and Clemmy near a rustic cart that was decked out with jugs of cider and barrels of apples. The smell alone was enough to draw Madeline to it and make her mouth water. "How's the cider stand?" she asked, walking up to them. She noticed nearly empty jugs.

"We're almost sold out," Clemmy said.

"I knew it would be a hit. Great job, you two."

Just as she was about to move on, she saw Anna, her face painted like a tiger running toward her with Jasmine trailing behind. Anna's eyes were wide with excitement as she held up a small chocolate cake. "Aunt Madeline, look! I won a cake at the cakewalk," she said.

Madeline bent down and pinched her cheek. "That's amazing, honey. You'll have to share a slice of that with me later. I'm going to be very hungry after this."

"Everything is looking so great, Madeline. You really outdid yourself," Jasmine said.

"Listen, it was not just me. Clemmy did a lot of the organizing for this, as did you. I'm just the one running around like a headless chicken, trying to make sure everything's okay."

Jasmine reached over and touched her arm. "Just make sure you enjoy it. After all, this is your first fall in Jubilee. It's a very magical time of the year."

"Thank you. I will."

The sun started to dip below the horizon, which cast a beautiful golden glow over the festival and the surrounding mountains. Madeline had been worried about this day for the last two weeks, but now that she saw it come together, she felt like she got the real reward.

As the rest of the evening passed, there was a hayride where Brady and Anna jumped onto the tractor and pulled children and parents around town. Jasmine ran a pumpkin carving station as well as apple bobbing. And Frannie, someone that Madeline had not officially met yet, was selling wonderful desserts outside of her new bakery that was soon to open.

At the end of it, Madeline was exhausted. As much as she had enjoyed herself, she was ready to go home and slip into a hot bath and then slide into bed.

As she stood there looking at the remnants of the Harvest Festival finishing up, she felt a hand slip into hers. It was Brady. "You really did great, Madeline," he said softly as he leaned into her ear.

"I had no idea what community really looked like until I moved to Jubilee, and now I can't imagine living anywhere else."

"Oh, really?" he said.

"Yeah. I think people who don't live in a small town like this have no idea what they're missing."

Brady pulled her close in a tight hug. "Well, I'm glad you found out because if you hadn't, I never would've met you." They stood there with their arms wrapped around each other as they looked at the town they both called home, and Madeline knew for sure that this was what life was supposed to be about.

As the festival came to a close and the lights dimmed, the chatter and laughter of the day's festivities started to fade into the backdrop. Frannie found herself standing alone, looking at the emptying grounds of the town square.

The Harvest Festival, as usual, had been a whirlwind of activity, and she was exhausted. She had never been quite so involved in it. Most of the time she was just a spectator, just a visitor. That was, if she even got to come. She didn't spend a lot of the fall at her grandmother's house except for the couple of years in high school where she lived with her full-time.

Her dessert booth had been a hit, and that gave her a glimmer of hope that maybe, just maybe, her bakery was going to be a success. It was a little scary being in such a small town. It was very easy for a business to fail if the community didn't get behind it. She didn't know why they wouldn't, but she wasn't one-hundred percent sure that she was going to be successful.

Cole walked over, his hands tucked into the pockets of his well-worn jeans. "Hey, Frannie, how'd it go? Did you give Jubilee a taste of what's to come?"

She looked at him and smiled. "You know, it went better than I expected. I sold out of everything. Those apple turnovers were the first to go."

"Well, they are fantastic," he said. "See, I told you this town needed a good bakery."

Frannie sighed, her shoulders slumping a little. "It's just a start, Cole. There is still so much more to do. The renovations, licenses, inspections, and that's not even thinking about the day-to-day running of the bakery. Sometimes I wonder what in the world I've gotten myself into."

His expression softened. "It's a big leap to go from being a nurse to running a bakery. I get that. But if anybody can pull it off, it's you."

She looked at him, touched by his confidence in her. "Thank you. It means a lot, especially coming from you. So, how's your dad? How's everything going on your end?"

His face clouded over for a moment. "It's tough. Actually, a lot tougher than I thought it was going to be. He's not the man he used to be, and it's hard for both of us, I think. I just don't want to let him down, you know?"

She nodded, understanding exactly what he meant. "Yes, the weight of expectations can be a heavy burden. I feel it, too."

"Yeah, I know you understand. Sometimes it's those very expectations that push us to be better than we ever thought we could be. At least that's what I tell myself every morning when I wake up and put on these work boots."

For a minute, neither of them spoke, each of them lost in their own thoughts and probably their own fears. But there was a comfort in the shared understanding they had. Finally, Cole broke the silence. "You know, Frannie, this town rallies around its own. You're not alone, and neither am I. We just have to remember that."

"I've missed this, Cole. Missed being a part of a community like this. I've missed these simple, yet deep connections. I didn't have that for so many years."

He took a step closer. "Then let's promise, no matter how tough things get, that we won't lose sight of why we came back to Jubilee."

She nodded. "That's a promise."

As they stood there, watching the rest of the people file out of the town square and the daylight fading, Frannie felt a renewed sense of purpose. Even though the road ahead was going to be uncertain and filled with challenges and obstacles, she felt optimistic about it. "Well, I'd better get home. I need to help my dad get ready for bed," Cole said, his eyes lingering on her face for a moment longer than necessary.

"Goodnight, Cole," she said, watching him walk away, his silhouette gradually blending into the twilight as if he walked straight into the dark mountains beyond. She stood there for a few more moments thinking about how blessed she was to have a community like Jubilee. If anywhere was going to be accepting of her and her new bakery, it was this place. Her Nana had the right idea when she called Jubilee home.

CHAPTER 7

The next day, Madeline was exhausted. She had slept late, written a little bit on her book, and then taken another nap. Much to her surprise, Geneva walked over right before dinnertime and invited Eloise to come to dinner at her house alone, without Madeline. It seemed odd, but Madeline was glad to have the time to herself.

As she watched her mother walk away with Geneva, she noticed a slight limp that she hadn't noticed before. Maybe she had just gotten overtired walking around at the festival. Putting it out of her mind, she went back into the house and opened the refrigerator, looking to see what she had left over. The last thing she wanted to do was prepare dinner. She was just too tired for that. Just as she was about to pull out some leftover spaghetti sauce that might have been just a little past its prime, she heard a tap at her door.

Oh, no. Her mother must be coming back. She had probably changed her mind before she even got to Geneva's driveway. Instead, she noticed somebody on her porch move away quickly. She walked over and peeked out to see if she could figure out who it was, but nobody was there. Instead, there was a simple, long stem red rose and an envelope laying on the welcome mat. She leaned over and picked it up, laying the rose on a side table just inside her front door so she could open the envelope. As soon as she saw it, she knew it was Brady's handwriting.

It said she was invited to dinner, to put on her most comfortable clothes, hop in the golf cart and meet him in the barn. She was intrigued, and she was already wearing her most comfortable clothes: her favorite pair of black yoga pants, a T-shirt with a picture of the mountains on it, and her black flats. She shut the door behind her and hopped into the golf cart, heading straight for his barn. She needed some time with Brady. It seemed like they were always going in different directions lately, and she missed those warm, cozy moments they'd had every day when he was living in her basement.

As she parked the golf cart, the sun was just

starting to set. She headed through the woods - which Brady had cleared out and made a path for her - and walked over to the barn. As she stepped through the weathered barn doors, her breath caught in her throat. Brady had transformed the space into an intimate cocoon of romance, a far cry from the tension-filled home that she'd left behind with her mother. He popped out in front of her, coming out of one of the side stalls, a smile on his handsome face. In his hands he held another eleven long-stem red roses. That's when she realized he had simply removed one and laid it on her front porch.

"Brady, this is ... It's like a dream," she said, her eyes starting to well with tears. He took her hand and led her further inside.

"You have been under so much stress lately. Your mom is visiting, and she's a handful. Planning a whole festival. Trying to finish a book. I just wanted to give you a break. Geneva was more than happy to take Eloise for the evening."

That's when Madeline realized what had happened. They had worked together to do this. She felt so grateful in that moment. The barn was awash with a soft golden glow coming from the candles that he had arranged all over the rustic wooden beams, and mason jars that he had somehow hung from the rafters, that were filled with twinkle lights. The flickering lights danced across their faces. The air was full of comforting sense of the fresh hay, the aged wood, and a hint of lavender. It all added to the romance. No one had ever done anything like this for Madeline.

In the center of the setting was a small table that had been elegantly set, covered in what appeared to be a vintage lace tablecloth. There was a bouquet of wildflowers in the center of it. Candles on the table were in crystal holders, and their light reflected a myriad of patterns across the top of the barn.

Brady pulled out her chair, and as she sat down, he leaned in and whispered. "I wanted tonight to be a sanctuary for us. A place where we can just forget everything going on around us and just be together."

They sat and ate a dinner that he had prepared: steak with garlic mashed potatoes and a side salad. As they ate and talked about the fall festival and what was going on in each of their lives, Madeline couldn't help but be thankful that she had a relationship like this. In her mid-fifties now, she never would've thought such a blessing would come. A second chance that she never knew was possible.

Every day that she woke up in Jubilee, she knew that it was the right choice for her. But if anyone had asked her a year ago whether she'd be living in some small town, on the side of a mountain, in a log home, or sitting in a barn eating dinner with the love of her life while a goat watched them, she would've told them they were crazy.

After they finished eating dinner, the soulful strains of Johnny Mathis singing "Misty" started to play from a stereo sitting on a table in the corner. Brady held out his hand.

"May I have this dance?"

Little did he know that was one of Madeline's favorite songs of all time. Possibly the most romantic song. And here she was in this candlelit barn with the love of her life about to have a slow dance. How did she get so lucky?

As they moved together, their bodies swaying in perfect harmony to the music, Madeline felt a sense of happiness and peace that she had never felt before.

"I didn't think it was possible to feel this loved," she said, looking up at him.

"And I never knew it was possible to love someone as much as I love you," Brady said.

In that moment, surrounded by the beauty he had created for her, and the beauty of the mountains God had created for them, Madeline knew that she had found her forever sanctuary in the arms of the man that she loved.

Madeline pulled the golf cart into the driveway, her heart still fluttering from the wonderful evening she'd spent with Brady. She had needed that like she needed air. The moon was hanging full in the sky, casting an ethereal glow over the mountains in the distance. As she walked towards the front porch, her eyes caught a silhouette rocking gently on the porch. It was her mother.

"Why are you sitting out here in the dark, Mom?" Madeline asked, her voice tinged with concern.

Eloise looked up, "I find the night soothing, especially here. The quiet gives me space to think. I don't get much of that back home."

Madeline hesitated for a moment, trying to figure out if she wanted to ruin her wonderful, romantic evening by having a conversation with her mom. In the end, she decided to join her and sat down in the rocking chair beside her, the wood creaking softly as she moved.

"Is everything okay?"

Eloise sighed, her eyes staring out into the

distance. "You know, since I came here, I've been doing some soul-searching, Madeline. I think I've been unfair to you."

"You do?" Madeline said, surprised.

"Sometimes I think I'm giving you good advice and feedback."

Madeline chuckled. "I'm sure you think that."

"If I have been critical of you, your lifestyle, things like that, it's because I simply don't understand it myself, but I think I have failed to see the beautiful life that you're building for yourself here."

Madeline felt her heart actually skip a beat. She had never heard her mother speak so openly. "What is bringing this on, Mom?"

Eloise turned to face her daughter, the moonlight casting a glow over her face. Madeline could see regret maybe mixed with a newfound understanding. "I had dinner with Geneva tonight. We talked a lot about you, about ourselves and about the importance of letting people live their own lives."

Madeline felt a lump forming in her throat. "Geneva has a way of getting to the heart of things. That's why I love her."

Eloise nodded, "She does. She made me realize that I might've been holding on to some of my own dreams for you, my own expectations, and that made me blind to the dreams that you had for yourself. It's hard being a mother sometimes. As a parent, we have preconceived notions as to who they're going to be, or what kind of life we hope they will lead. In the end, though, it's our hopes and dreams we have projected on them, and not necessarily what our child wanted, and no child can live up to that expectation. No child is ever going to be exactly like their parents think they're going to be."

"I'm glad you've realized that," Madeline said. "And I think if you just give it a chance, you'll understand why I chose the career that I did."

Eloise laughed, "I don't know if I'll ever understand that. To be honest, I've watched you interact with Geneva since I've gotten here, and I might've been a little jealous of that."

"Jealous? Why?"

"Because I've always wanted that kind of connection with you, Madeline, and it's been hard since you became an adult, since your father left."

"Can I ask you something, Mom?"

"Of course."

"You were a different person before dad left. It seemed after he was gone, you became more critical, more pessimistic, more argumentative at times."

"I suppose that's true. There's a lot of stuff I don't

think I ever dealt with. My generation just pulled ourselves up by our bootstraps and moved on."

"Well, I think that might be part of the problem. You didn't move on. You became somebody that I didn't recognize, somebody I had to pull away from. It was hurtful and painful not to have you in my life."

"I understand, it was painful for me too. I didn't understand why you were pulling away. I don't think I ever really got it until I came here and heard some of the things coming out of my mouth. I'm never going to be perfect, Madeline."

"And I don't expect you to be. I really don't. But, I do expect you to respect the life I've chosen for myself, and I hope you can just be happy for me, even if you don't understand it completely."

"I'm going to try. I promise you that. And, as far as me changing after your father left, I did. I thought I would be with him forever. He really pulled the rug out from under me and you. It just made me not trust anyone. It made me see the world in a negative way. I know I need to work on that, even at my age."

Madeline reached over and put her hand on her mother's. "You can do it. You can have a second chance. It doesn't matter what your age is."

"I hope you're right. I really do," she said, turning

and staring back at the mountains. Although it was dark, lights dotted them and the moon lit up the sky.

"You know, I love this town, Mom," Madeline said softly. "I love the people, the sense of the community, the simple way of life. I love Brady, and I see a future here."

"And that's what truly matters, Madeline. If you're happy, genuinely happy, then I need to learn to be happy for you."

"So, does this mean you're going to give Jubilee a chance?"

Eloise squeezed Madeline's hand gently, “Yes, and I’m giving us a chance, a chance to rebuild our relationship, to understand each other better, and maybe to be a part of each other's lives in a meaningful way."

"That's all I've ever wanted."

They sat there, hand in hand, rocking on the porch under the soft glow of the moonlight. Madeline couldn't believe how this evening had gone. First, a wonderfully romantic date with the love of her life and now a reconciliation attempt by her mother. It was a small step, but it was a step forward. "I'm pretty tired. Brady had me dancing under the twinkle lights for quite some time," Madeline said, standing up.

"I'm glad you had a nice evening. I like him. He seems like a good man."

"Are you coming inside?" Madeline asked.

"In a minute. I just want to enjoy this last little bit of time, but I'll see you in the morning."

"Goodnight, Mom," Madeline said as she turned and headed toward the house, still hearing the creaking of her mother's rocking chair behind her. Maybe this was the day that she got a new beginning with her mother. At least, that's what she hoped.

Frannie stood in the middle of what would soon become her brand new bakery. She didn't have a name picked out yet, which was a problem because she needed to get the sign made. She had been thinking about it and scratching ideas out onto a notepad before tossing them in the trash can almost daily. Her eyes scanned the walls that still needed to be painted, but at least she had the rustic wooden tables already, and Cole was hanging some shelving on one of the brick walls. The bakery was coming together, and she couldn't help but feel a sense of pride mixed with anticipation.

"Almost done," Cole said, stepping back to admire his handiwork. "What do you think?"

"They're perfect, Cole. They're going to look great once I fill them up."

He wiped his brow and smiled. "Well, we do have one more thing we need to test. That new oven. Are you ready to fire it up?"

She smiled. "Absolutely. How about we christen it by baking Nana's famous chocolate cake?"

Cole's eyes lit up. "Oh, I remember that cake. It was the stuff of legends in Jubilee."

Frannie walked over to a box that had been sitting on one of the tables and pulled out the worn handwritten recipe card. "I've got the recipe right here. Nana would be excited to know that her cake is the first thing I'm going to bake in my brand new oven."

They gathered up the ingredients: flour, sugar, cocoa powder, eggs, and the rest. Frannie put on her apron, and Cole followed suit. They stood there side by side, measuring and mixing, the chemistry between them just as present as it ever was.

"Okay, time for the cocoa powder," Frannie said, reaching over for the container. But just as she was about to pour it, Cole bumped into her and a cloud of cocoa powder erupted above them, covering them both. Frannie burst into laughter, which was a welcome relief given the amount of stress she'd experienced recently. Her face and apron were dusted with cocoa. Cole looked equally comical with chocolate smudges all over his face.

"I am so sorry," Cole said, trying not to laugh.

Frannie playfully swiped her finger across his cheek, leaving the only clean area on it. "You look pretty good in chocolate," she teased, before licking her finger. The room seemed to freeze, the tension thickening.

He looked into her eyes, his gaze intense, yet tender. "I could say the same thing about you." For a moment, they stood there, the air thick with unsaid words and unresolved feelings. It seemed that there was about to be a romantic moment when Frannie suddenly broke the silence.

"We should finish this cake."

Cole nodded, clearing his throat. "Right, right. The cake."

They resumed their baking, this time managing to avoid any other disasters in the kitchen. As they poured the batter into the pan and slid it into the oven, Frannie felt a sense of excitement wash over her. She was doing this. She was really doing it. She was going to open her own bakery and honor her grandmother's legacy and fulfill their dream. When the oven timer dinged, they both jumped. Cole pulled the cake out of the oven. Its rich chocolate aroma filling the entire space. "It looks perfect," Frannie said.

Cole looked at her, his eyes soft. "No, Frannie, you're perfect. Your Nana would be so proud of what you're doing, and I'm honored to be a part of this."

“I’m not perfect, but thank you," she said not knowing what else to say. There weren't enough words. As she looked at the cake cooling on the wire rack, she turned to Cole, who was busy wiping down the counters, trying to clean things up from the chocolate explosion. "Cole..." she began.

He turned around looking at her. "Yeah?"

"I wanted to thank you. Not just for the bakery, but just for being here, for coming back into my world when you did. It's been a whirlwind, and I don't think I could have done any of this without you."

"I should be thanking you, Frannie. Coming back to Jubilee to take care of my dad, well, it's been a lot, and helping you with this bakery has given me something to look forward to every day. I'm going to miss it when we're finished."

She took a step closer. "I have missed you, Cole.

All these years I've thought about what went wrong between us. Why did you ever leave without saying goodbye?" It was the question she had been wanting to ask this entire time, but it seemed so pointless after so many years apart. After all, she had been married and now divorced. It wasn't like she was pining for her high school sweetheart every day, but she did think about him often and she wondered what happened.

Cole looked down at her, his face a mix of regret and sorrow.

"Frannie, I feel like I owe you an explanation. Honestly, I should have contacted you years ago, but I didn't know if you were married or what was going on in your life. I didn't want to disrupt anything. But when we were in high school, what you didn't know was that my family was going through a really tough time financially. So, when I got my scholarship, I felt like my sole focus had to be on helping them by making the most of my opportunity. I was just a kid, and I thought that if I did well in school, that I could somehow help my parents. I thought that I was doing the responsible thing by letting you go so that you could have the freedom you needed in college. But, I guess the truth is I was scared myself; I was scared of failing you, failing my parents. I was scared of holding you back. I convinced myself in my stupid, immature male mind that it was for the best. But, all these years, not a day has gone by that I haven't regretted that decision. I should have been honest with you way back then, and I'm really sorry for any pain that I caused you."

"You know, I waited for you. I thought you'd come back. When I realized you weren't going to, I left Jubilee. It was hard to come back to even visit my grandmother for a long time."

"I'm sorry. I can only say I'm sorry. I wish I could change it."

She smiled slightly. "I've often wondered over the years how things might've been different if we'd stayed together, if we'd gotten married and had a family."

"I've thought about that myself," Cole said, looking at her intensely.

"I mean, I did eventually get married and now I'm divorced. No kids. I feel like I sort of wasted a lot of time in my twenties."

"But, did you learn about yourself? Did you learn what you want and what you don't want?"

"Yes, I definitely did."

"Well, then maybe it was worth it because now

when you get what you want, you'll appreciate it. You'll work hard, and you'll never let it go."

"I guess you're right. I'm already appreciating everything that has happened since I came back to Jubilee."

"I'm glad you're back. It feels like a new beginning," Cole said. "I mean for you. For the bakery."

"Right. For the bakery." She turned so he couldn't see her eyes welling with tears. Was there a possibility that he might want a second chance at romance with her, or was he just being a good friend? Frannie was afraid to ask that question.

CHAPTER 8

Madeline sat at her rustic Amish kitchen table with a blank notebook in front of her and a pen in her hand. She kept getting distracted by the beautiful mountain view out of the windows in front of her, or maybe it was just because she was procrastinating. This was one of the hardest tasks she'd ever done, and after just having helped with the harvest festival a few weeks ago, now this seemed even more insurmountable.

The table was strewn with cookbooks, recipes handwritten by Geneva, and a few printouts from the Internet that she'd found, but she still stared at an empty page, her mind racing with thoughts of turkeys, roast beef, and peach cobbler.

"Okay, you can do this," she said to herself, taking a deep breath. "You've sold millions of books to readers around the world. You've hosted dinner parties before. This is just Thanksgiving dinner."

No matter what she said to herself, it didn't seem to make a difference. The stakes just felt completely higher, which was ridiculous because everybody coming to her Thanksgiving dinner cared about her. Nobody was coming to write a review to publish in the newspaper.

She started to jot down her menu, her handwriting a little shaky at first, but she grew more confident as she went along. Just then, she heard some creaking behind her as her mother walked into the room. The hardwood floors always gave anyone away. There was no sneaking up on anyone in a log home built on the side of a mountain.

"Planning a feast, are you?" Eloise asked.

"Yes. You know it's my first time cooking Thanksgiving dinner. I just want it to be perfect. I think I'm a little overwhelmed, to be honest."

Eloise hesitated for a moment, but then took a step closer.

"Do you want some help?"

Madeline looked at her mother, her eyes searching for a catch, but all she really saw was sincerity. Since their conversation that night on the porch, things had been better. Her mom was still critical at points, but she usually caught herself. Madeline still had no idea why she arrived on her front porch or how long she was staying, but she was enjoying her company more than she ever had as an adult.

"I would actually love that, Mom," Madeline said, her voice tinged with relief.

Eloise sat down in the chair next to her and looked at the menu Madeline had written so far.

"This, it looks wonderful, but it sure is a lot for one person to handle."

"I know. Geneva and Clemmy said they'll bring a few things and Brady's handling the cooking of his grandmother's yeast rolls, but it's still a lot."

Eloise took the pen and started to write in the notebook. "Why don't we divide and conquer? I'll help you with the turkey and the salad. You can focus on the roast beef, and we'll share the sides."

Madeline felt a weight lift off her shoulders. "That honestly sounds like a great plan. Besides, I remember how good your turkey is."

Eloise smiled. "Well, then it's settled. We're going to be cooking Thanksgiving dinner together. Boy, I never thought I'd hear myself say that."

"Me neither," Madeline said, laughing. "But I'm

glad things are changing between us. It feels good to have you here, especially for the holidays."

"I'm glad I have a place to be. You know, as you get older and your family and friends start to pass away, you always worry that you might be the last one standing. That every Christmas or Thanksgiving or any other holiday might be the one where you're alone. I certainly have friends who are alone during the holidays and pretty much every other day of the year."

"That's really sad, Mom. I'm sorry to hear that."

"Well, when you live in a retirement community, everybody's kids have flown the coop. Sometimes they don't come back."

Madeline reached over and touched her hand. "Well, I'm back. We're back together, so you don't have to worry about being alone for the holidays or any other time. I'm here."

"I appreciate that, I really do. And I have to say I've enjoyed everyone I've met here so far. Even if this isn't the place I necessarily would have picked to live when I showed up here, I'm starting to see the allure."

"You mean Jubilee is starting to grow on you?" Madeline asked, smiling.

"A little," Eloise said, holding up two fingers about an inch apart.

"Good. I think I'm going to go take a shower and then maybe we can head over to the grocery store to start getting everything we need."

"Of course. I'll wait down here and be ready to go."

As Madeline walked upstairs, she thought about how far her relationship with her mother had come. Even though she still didn't totally trust her reason for showing up that day, she was glad that she did.

Madeline was a little worried about taking her mother grocery shopping at Maynard's. After all, the grocery store was decades old, very small, and not at all what her mother was probably accustomed to. But a few days before Thanksgiving, they had no choice. Madeline and Eloise found themselves bustling through the aisles, trying to get a few last-minute things. Their cart was already half full with fresh vegetables, a big bag of flour, cartons of broth and the requisite cans of cranberry sauce. As far as Brady was concerned, cranberry sauce came from a can and needed to be can shaped. He wasn't going to eat it any other way. Madeline laughed every time she thought about it.

As they walked down the aisle in the produce section, Madeline picked up a bag of peaches, looking at each of them carefully before placing them into the cart. "These will be perfect for the cobbler."

Eloise nodded. "Do we have enough cinnamon and nutmeg?"

"I think so, but you can never be too safe. Grab an extra bottle of each. We can always use them."

They moved through the store, and Madeline couldn't help but feel a sense of camaraderie with her mother. That was something she had not felt in many years. They talked about different cooking ideas, debated the merits of the canned versus fresh cranberry sauce, and even laughed over a display in the store of novelty turkey-shaped salt and pepper shakers. Madeline wanted to get some, but Eloise said they were tacky and she should leave them out of the buggy.

Finally, they reached the meat section, and Madeline carefully selected a roast. In her stressed-out mentality, Madeline had forgotten to get a turkey days ago when she was doing her normal shopping. She was surprised any were still available, but thankfully they got lucky and grabbed one of the last ones that were there.

They finally made their way to the checkout, and as Madeline looked at their cart, which was filled to the brim with the makings of a perfect Thanksgiving dinner, she felt a sense of happiness wash over her. Before her mother had shown up, she didn't realize how much she had missed having her in her life. There was such a wall around her when it came to her mother that she didn't think about it. She didn't even allow herself to feel the feelings of loss that were so obviously there. Now, all she felt was happiness. Occasionally, her mother would say or do something that would want to send her reeling, but she came back to the conversation they had that night in the rocking chairs. Knowing her mother was at least trying was more than she could ask for and was certainly something she was thankful for this year.

"Thank you, Mom," she said softly as they waited in line. "This means a lot to me."

Eloise reached over and squeezed her hand. "It means a lot to me too, Madeline. I'm so happy we get to do this together this year. I will have a lot to be thankful for when we eat this meal."

"Well, hello, ladies," Clemmy said as she walked

through the front door and met them near the checkout.

"Hey, Clemmy. Are you coming in to get some last-minute things?"

"Oh, yes. As usual, there's always something to get at the grocery store when you're cooking for Thanksgiving. I'm so happy I'm getting to come to your house this year, Madeline. It would've been awfully lonely if I didn't have anywhere to go."

"We're glad you get to come too," Madeline said, handing her mother the credit card to pay for the groceries as she stepped over to the side to continue her conversation with Clemmy.

"Now, I hope you don't mind that I'm going to make a couple of my favorite Thanksgiving side dishes."

"Oh, definitely. I don't mind at all," Madeline said. "I can use the help for sure. What are you planning to bring?"

"Well, I'd like to bring a sweet potato casserole, and I also have a great green bean casserole I was planning to bring."

"Oh, those both sound wonderful. I talked to Geneva this morning, and she said she's going to make her famous baked mac and cheese and she's got a wonderful chocolate pecan pie that will knock your socks off."

Madeline's mouth watered. "I can't wait. I was feeling pretty overwhelmed and stressed having to cook this dinner, but with everybody chipping in, I think I might actually have a relaxing day," Madeline said, laughing.

Clemmy reached out and grabbed both of her hands. "Honey, this is going to be so much fun. I'm so blessed that you moved to Jubilee when you did. I never thought I might find a new friend at my age."

Madeline smiled. "Neither did I, Clemmy. Neither did I."

It was a quiet evening for Frannie. Most evenings were quiet. Ever since her divorce, she was having to get used to being alone again. Not that her marriage was all that great. Her husband traveled for work and probably did a lot of other things while he was out of town and away from her prying eyes. She tried not to think about it. What she did know about him was enough to divorce him, and she tried not to waste her time thinking anymore of it.

Now in her thirties, it felt weird to be alone all the time. This wasn't exactly where she thought she'd be at this stage in her life. As she dipped her paintbrush into the soft blue hue, her eyes squinting as she focused on the wall in front of her, Frannie thought back to what her original dreams were when she left high school.

She'd wanted to be married, she'd wanted to be a nurse, and she'd wanted to have children. She'd wanted to go to parent-teacher conferences. She'd wanted to go to the playground and push her children in the swings. She'd wanted to wake up on Christmas morning and surprise them with everything that Santa Claus had brought the night before.

But instead, she found herself alone every day and every night. And as much as she tried not to feel sorry for herself, she couldn't help it. As much as she tried to be the strong independent-minded woman that she was, she still missed having a husband and children. She missed having a family, and she didn't know if it was ever going to happen for her. Moving to Jubilee didn't mean she was going to be in the middle of a great singles scene, after all, but at least the bakery was coming together. And tonight she was working on the walls -the last big project.

Anxious thoughts swirled around in her brain. She sighed as she thought about the budget and how she'd gone over it. She thought about the upcoming health inspection and the mountain of other tasks that she still needed to do, and just as she was about to lay on the floor in the fetal position, the front door creaked open. She turned to see Cole stepping inside. He was holding an insulated bag and a couple of bottles of water in his hand. He smiled. "I thought maybe you could use some company and some dinner."

Frannie's heart skipped a beat. "You didn't have to do that, but I'm so glad you did. I'm starving. What did you bring?"

"I brought chicken parmesan sandwiches from that little Italian place that we used to go to in high school. You know, the one behind the library? I remembered it was one of your favorites, right?"

She set her paintbrush down and wiped her hands on a rag. "I can't believe you remembered that."

He shrugged, a sheepish grin on his face. "Well, some things are hard to forget." He set the bag and drinks on one of the wooden tables that would soon become the place bakery customers ate delectable sweets. He pulled the sandwiches out, both of them wrapped in foil and opened the two bottles of water.

Frannie pulled a couple of mismatched chairs

over, and they sat down. Surprisingly, Cole retrieved a small candle out of his pocket and lit it, placing it in the center of the table. She didn't know where the candle came from, but it felt awfully romantic that he had it in his pocket. Maybe she was overthinking things. They unwrapped their sandwiches and for a few moments they ate in silence.

Finally, Cole spoke. "So you were a nurse before this, right? That's a pretty big leap. The medical field to a bakery."

She nodded. "It is, but it's something I've always wanted to do, especially with my grandmother. But now that Nana is gone, I feel like I'm doing it for both of us. Nursing was a fulfilling career, but it was very draining. And then I went through a divorce and that made me really reevaluate what I wanted in my life."

"I'm sorry to hear about your divorce. I'm sure that was tough. I've never been married, so I can't quite understand it."

"It's life. We were never right for each other. I think I always knew that deep down, but I settled anyway because I wanted a family. Turns out we ended up not even having a family. He kept delaying it, and now I know it was because he wasn't sure about us either. And then I've spent a lot of time recently just thinking about all the choices I've made in my life, some of the opportunities that I've missed."

"Like us?" Cole ventured.

She looked at him. "Yes, like us. You broke my heart, Cole. We were kids, but it was real for me."

He put his sandwich down. "I know. I don't think I could ever tell you I'm sorry enough. I was young and stupid, and it was the worst decision I've ever made. Don't you think it is weird that we're suddenly back in each other's lives after all these years?" Without warning, he reached across the table, his fingers lightly touching hers. "I've thought about you a lot over the years and wondered what you were up to, if you were happy. I wanted to reach out so many times, but if you were married, I didn't want to interfere. When I moved back here to take over my dad's business, I never expected to find you here. But now that I have, I really don't want to waste another moment wondering 'what if.'" She felt her eyes misting over. She was touched but also very scared. She felt those old feelings for Cole stronger than ever. Sometimes she wondered if they were just those old feelings from high school or if they were real adult feelings. Either way, she was afraid of getting hurt all over again.

He seemed to sense her hesitation. "Listen, Frannie, I can't change the past, but what I can promise you is that I'm not a scared kid anymore. I'm here in Jubilee and I'm not leaving, and I would really like to see where this could go if you would be willing to take that chance."

She looked into his eyes and saw so much sincerity there. For the first time since high school, she felt a warmth flowing through her chest that felt like home. Maybe it was time to take a chance on herself and on her future. "What do you mean exactly?"

"Well, I think it would be great if after you open this bakery and you have an evening free, maybe I could take you on a date?"

She smiled slightly. "Okay, Cole, let's take that chance." As they sat there with the candle flickering between them, Frannie felt a sense of hope and excitement that she hadn't felt in so many years. Somehow God had conspired to bring them back together in Jubilee, and she hoped that it was the beginning of a bright new future she never could have expected.

CHAPTER 9

It was two days before Thanksgiving, and it wasn't like Madeline didn't have anything to do. She had a book deadline looming, which she had already gotten an extension for, a Thanksgiving dinner to prepare, and the relationship with her mother to continue mending. But when she got a phone call earlier that morning from Geneva inviting her to a local winery with Clemmy, she just couldn't say no.

Madeline loved wine, and she hadn't gotten to visit any of the wineries that dotted the Blue Ridge Mountain area. As she pulled into the gravel parking lot, she spotted Geneva's car. They could have carpooled, but Geneva was already in town at the bookstore when she and Clemmy decided to take a little day trip. Madeline got out of her car and took a deep breath, relishing in the fresh air. Geneva and Clemmy were already seated at a table overlooking the mountains on the outdoor patio, a bottle of red wine and three glasses in front of them.

"There she is," Geneva exclaimed, standing up and giving Madeline a hug. "We thought you might could use this today."

"You have no idea," Madeline said, taking a seat. "This book is going to be the end of me."

"You're not finding it easy to write about small town life yet?" Geneva asked.

"It's not that it's hard; it's just that it's different. I'm having to change the way I describe things. Anyway, it's just taking me longer than normal. I've already asked for one extension, so I have to get it finished."

"Well, for right now, we want you to sit back and relax, and enjoy the beautiful views," Clemmy said, pouring her a glass and sliding it over to her.

Madeline took a sip, savoring the rich, fruity flavor. "You know, you ladies are my lifesavers. I feel like I'm drowning in responsibilities."

Geneva leaned over, "Dear, you can't pour from an empty cup, you know. Sometimes you just have to step back and take care of yourself."

Madeline nodded. "I know, but it's easier said

than done. With Thanksgiving dinner and trying to figure out what to do with my mother sometimes, it's just been a lot."

Clemmy sighed. "Relationships, I've found, can be tricky. Take me, for instance. My grown son is in the military, and I know he's busy, but I don't hear from him nearly as much as I'd like. It can be hurtful, and sometimes we just take things to heart too much. I miss him like I miss my teenage waistline, but I have to give him grace because I know he's got important stuff to do."

"I'm sorry you're missing your son," Madeline said.

"I totally agree," Geneva interjected. "I've never had children of my own, but I know how easy it is to take something that a person says or does and think that it's directed at us. Sometimes, it's just more about them. Madeline, I think what your mother has been going through all these years is more about her than it is about you."

Madeline nodded. "I think you're right. Now that we've had a chance to talk more, I feel like she realizes some of the things that she's said and done over the years have been hurtful to me. I'm hoping that our relationship will continue to get better, and I'm actually glad that she's here. I didn't think I would say that a few weeks ago when she showed up on my front porch."

Geneva and Clemmy laughed. "Well, to totally change the subject, I want to ask you for a favor," Clemmy said.

Madeline looked at her, glaring. "The last favor you asked me for resulted in me organizing an entire fall festival, so I'm a little hesitant to say yes before I hear the details."

"It's nothing big. I'm going to have a little Christmas event right after Thanksgiving at the bookstore. I thought maybe you might like to set up a table and sign some books."

"Oh, of course. I'm always willing to do that. I used to love going to book signings. I would jump on a plane or in my car and show up at some random bookstore across the country. But, these days I don't really want to leave Jubilee. So, coming to your place is perfect."

"Well, good! I'm glad that I get to be the beneficiary of you not wanting to leave town or your super cute boyfriend behind."

Madeline waved her hand. "I didn't say anything about Brady."

"We all know you love him," Geneva said. "Both of you get googly eyes at each other."

"You ladies are going to make me blush," Madeline said laughing. "And I'm too old to be blushing."

"You're never too old to fall in love."

"Oh, really? And have you thought about falling in love again?" Clemmy asked.

"Okay, maybe you can be too old to fall in love," Geneva said, smacking her leg and laughing. "I'm too set in my ways to let a man back into my life. My husband was a wonderful person, but he would leave the toilet seat up, and sometimes I'd have to nag him to pull the weeds in the front yard. I don't want to start dealing with that again."

Madeline giggled. "Are you saying that Brady might start leaving the toilet seat up at some point?"

"You never know," Geneva said, wagging her finger.

"So anyway, back to the book signing. I would love to do it, Clemmy. Just send me the details, and I'll bring a big stack of books."

"Thank you. I appreciate you doing this so much. Now let's stop talking about work, mothers and men, and let's drink as much of this wine as we can without getting into trouble," Geneva said.

Frannie pushed open the door to Perky's Coffee Shop, the little bell above the door ringing and letting everyone in town know that she had arrived. The smell of freshly brewed coffee felt like a warm hug, instantly comforting her. As she walked in, Perky looked up from behind the counter and smiled.

"Frannie, my dear, come sit down. I've got a fresh pot of hazelnut brewed that will warm you to your very core."

Frannie smiled and waved. "That sounds fantastic."

She walked over and sat down at one of the tables near the window overlooking the mountains. She would never get tired of that view. Even though it was the same view of the mountains every day, it always looked different. The shadows and shades of the sunlight and darkness against the blue hills always provided a totally different picture, and then when you added in the different seasons, it was like looking at a new painting all throughout the day.

A few minutes later, Perky joined her at the table, setting down two steaming mugs of coffee and a plate of peach fritters.

"I swear, if you don't stop giving me pastries

every time I come in here, I'm going to be as big as the side of a barn." Frannie said, laughing. "Plus, I'm now going to own a bakery. I guess I should join some sort of weight loss support group right now."

Perky laughed, "Honey, life is for enjoying things. Don't ever feel bad about the calories. Happy calories are free calories. Anyway, let's talk about the grand opening. I was thinking, maybe we could do a little cross-promotion with each other. Maybe I could sell some of your pastries here, and you could offer my coffee over at the bakery."

Frannie grinned. "You know, that sounds like a great idea, Perky. I mean, it is a win-win for both of us."

"Exactly. Now, for that grand opening party, what kind of entertainment were you thinking about? My grandson plays the guitar. He's very good and would be thrilled to perform."

"I really like that idea. Perhaps some Christmas music?" Frannie said, her mind was racing with various plans. "Maybe we could have some free samples. Since we're going into the Christmas season, I could create a little menu with all kinds of holiday themed baked goods."

"That's a fantastic idea," Perky said. "You know, people can't resist free samples. Every time I put out little free sample cups of coffee here, they're gone in a flash. Once they taste your baking, they will be hooked. You got that talent from your grandmother."

They continued to brainstorm, writing down ideas on a notepad Frannie had brought with her. After a little while, Perky put down her pen and looked at Frannie.

"Now, we've talked enough about business. How are things going with you and Cole?"

Frannie's cheeks felt like they were on fire. "Actually, pretty good. He brought me dinner the other night while I was painting. But, the whole thing is also very complicated."

Perky leaned across the table. "Well, the heart has its own timeline, doesn't it? What's bothering you?"

Frannie sighed, her finger tracing the rim of her coffee mug. "To be honest, I'm just scared, Perky. I don't want to get my heart broken again, and I'm not talking about my marriage. When Cole left me all those years ago after high school, I never got over it. I mean, it seems really silly to say that now that I'm an adult."

"Dear, my husband and I fell in love when we were very young. We didn't get married until some years later, but the love was there just the same, and

I can promise you, if he had left me, I would've never forgotten him."

"Well, that's exactly what happened to me. I got married, I settled for someone that wasn't right for me, and now here I am, divorced. So I'm not worried about getting my heart broken again like my divorce. I'm worried about getting my heart broken again like when Cole left me behind."

"So what are you going to do then?"

"Well, Cole and I have decided to give it another try. Take it slowly, of course. But what if it doesn't work out? What if his father gets worse or passes away, and Cole leaves town again?"

Perky reached across the table and covered Frannie's hand with her own. "Darling, love is always a risk, but I think it's a risk worth taking. You know, Eddie and I have been married for fifty years now, and let me tell you something. It hasn't always been smooth sailing, but we have weathered those storms together because we made a choice to do that, and love is a choice you make every single day. See, people think love is a feeling, but it's not. It's a commitment."

Frannie looked at her. "So, you're saying that you think I should go for it?"

Perky smiled, her eyes crinkling at the corners.

"I'm saying that life is too short for what ifs. If you don't give it a chance with Cole, if you don't take the second chance you've been given, and you know that he loves you and you love him, then you're always going to regret that you didn't take the chance. Don't let fear hold you back. My grandmother used to say, 'Take the leap and build your wings on the way down.'"

Frannie laughed at that saying. It sounded terrifying, but she was getting a new sense of courage while she talked to Perky. She hoped that it held.

"I think you're right. I need to take the chance, as scary as it might be, because if I don't, I don't think I can live with myself."

"And you just remember that I'm always here. I know you miss your nana, and you always will. She was a good woman, and she gave good advice, but I'm here too. I'm always going to be here to catch you if you fall. But something tells me you're not going to need that."

"Thank you, Perky. Coming back to Jubilee has made me realize just how much I needed a community of people around me. I'm finally starting to believe in myself again, and I can't wait to see what happens with this bakery and with Cole."

Madeline stood in the cozy kitchen of her beautiful mountain home, surrounded by the comforting scents of cinnamon and roasting turkey. She looked through the windows out over the mountains, watching a flock of crows fly across the bright blue sky. Wasn't a group of crows called a murder? Whoever came up with that? These were not the thoughts of someone on Thanksgiving, but she was an author and that's what went through an author's head sometimes.

She glanced at the clock. It was still pretty early. The guests would not be arriving for at least another couple of hours. She looked over at her mother, who was carefully peeling some potatoes.

"You're doing a great job with those potatoes," Madeline said smiling, as she stirred the gravy on the stove.

Eloise looked up and laughed. "Well, I've had a few decades of practice. I made you mashed potatoes many a time when you were little."

Madeline walked over to the island and placed a bowl of green beans next to her mother. "Would you mind snapping these for me when you're done with that?" Even though Clemmy was bringing green bean casserole, Eloise had still requested plain green beans, too. Madeline thought it was a little much but decided not to argue about it.

"Of course, dear," Eloise said, putting the peeled potatoes aside and picking up a handful of green beans. Madeline had watched her mother snap green beans many times as a child. Before that, she'd watched her grandmother. She supposed it was something that southern women just did, and she wondered if mothers in other parts of the country did the same thing.

For a few moments, the only sounds in the kitchen were the snap of beans and the simmer of the gravy on the stove. Madeline felt peaceful today. She loved these moments where nothing was wrong, everything was right, and she had only good things to look forward to. She had finished her book that morning, and it was off to the editor, so that was another big weight off of her shoulders for the holiday season.

She'd been so worried about how this Thanksgiving was going to go, especially with her mother being involved, but now they were working side by side in the kitchen, and she had to admit it felt nice.

"So, Mom," Madeline said, breaking the silence, "I noticed that you've been enjoying your time in

Jubilee, and you even volunteered to sell raffle tickets at the festival a few weeks ago."

"Yes, I did. And you know what? It was actually pretty fun. Geneva was a hoot to work with. She doesn't have much of a filter between her brain and her mouth. I have to say, I like that in a woman."

Madeline laughed. "Yes, Geneva has a certain effect on people. She's like the town's unofficial therapist."

"I can see that. She told me some stories about when you first moved here. Said you were like a fish out of water."

"I was definitely like a fish out of water, and I still am a lot of the time. Brady likes to laugh at me sometimes."

"Geneva told me that when you first moved here, you found a scorpion in the kitchen sink."

"Oh, yes, and she had to come over and show me how to stab it. Thankfully, I haven't seen another one. But if I do, I won't be stabbing it. I'll just be calling Geneva."

Eloise laughed. "How did you meet Brady?"

"Well, the morning I met Brady was right after I moved here. I was upset and didn't want to be here in the first place. I'm sound asleep and get woken up by the sound of gunshots."

"Gunshots? What on earth?"

"Well, it turned out he was skeet shooting, but I didn't know that at the time. I was so mad that he was interrupting my morning that I got in the golf cart and just drove straight down to his property."

"So let me get this straight. You heard the sound of gunshots, and you raced toward them? Haven't I ever taught you that's not the right thing to do?" Eloise said laughing.

"Yeah. Looking back on it now, I probably would've made a more rational decision, but in those times I was exhausted. I was worried about my career, and I didn't want to be in Jubilee at all."

"Well, it seems like you've adjusted now. You look very at home here, Madeline."

"I am. This town, these people, they've become my home."

"Honestly, I can see why," Eloise said, stopping and looking at her daughter. "There's a warmth here that's hard to explain. There's a sense of community that's really hard to find these days. There's a sense of family even when you aren't biologically related to somebody."

Madeline felt her heart swelling. This was the most that her mother had acknowledged her life in

Jubilee. "I'm glad you're seeing that, Mom. It really means a lot to me."

"Well, it's taken some time, but I'm getting there."

"So, how much longer do you plan to stay?"

Eloise laughed, "Are you trying to get rid of me?"

"No, but I've just never seen you leave your home for this long."

Eloise paused for a moment, "It's been a long time since you and I have been able to spend time together, and I didn't want to be alone for the holidays. So, I hope you don't mind if I stay until after Christmas."

"Of course, Mom. You're welcome to stay as long as you want."

Madeline felt herself making that promise and wondering if she was going to regret it. They were getting along right now, but was it because of the festivities of the holiday season? Was her mom just feeling more sentimental than normal?

Just then, the oven timer dinged, and Madeline put on her oven mitts. She carefully pulled out the roast beef, setting it up on the stovetop to rest.

"That looks and smells amazing," Eloise said.

"Yes, it does. This is actually Brady's grandmother's recipe."

"Oh, that's wonderful. I'm sure he'll be glad to taste it again."

"I just hope I did it justice," Madeline said laughing.

"You know, I wish I'd taught you more about cooking when you were growing up. We never had any moments like this."

"Well, we're having a moment now, Mom, and that's a memory we can cherish forever."

"Yes, you're right. And I wouldn't trade this time with you for the world."

Madeline suddenly felt the urge to hug her mother, which was something she hadn't done much as an adult. She walked over and hugged her tightly, grateful for this time they were getting to spend together. They just stood there in the kitchen, embraced in the warmth of everything around them. Madeline was so grateful, and she realized that's what Thanksgiving is about. It's about family, love, and maybe even some second chances. And right now, she felt like that's what she was getting, a second chance to be Eloise's daughter.

CHAPTER 10

A couple of hours later, the doorbell rang, and Madeline's heart leaped out of her chest with excitement and anxiousness. She smoothed her apron as she walked to the front door and swung it open to find Brady standing there, a warm smile on his face. He also had a basket of his grandmother's homemade yeast rolls in his hands.

"Happy Thanksgiving, beautiful," he said, as he leaned over to give her a kiss on the cheek.

"Happy Thanksgiving," she said, "Come on in. It's very chilly out there today." Brady stepped inside, followed by Jasmine who was carrying a dish of candied yams, and Anna, who held a pumpkin pie in her little hands. Clemmy and Geneva pulled up right afterwards, each of them carrying their own contributions to the dinner.

"I guess the gang's all here," Madeline said, taking each of their coats and hanging them on a coat rack near the door. The cabin was large but cozy, filled with the warm glow of lit candles, each of them emitting comforting scents of coffee or pumpkins. The fireplace was crackling, casting dancing shadows on the walls. Madeline had spent days adding rustic fall decor to set the scene.

"Wow, this place looks really amazing," Geneva said, looking around, "You've done a great job decorating it for fall."

"Thanks, Geneva. I just wanted it to feel warm and welcoming, especially today."

"Well, mission accomplished," Clemmy said, putting her green bean casserole on the kitchen counter next to an array of other delicious-looking dishes. Anna's eyes were wide and filled with wonder. As she looked around the room, she spotted Eloise, who was coming out of the kitchen holding a tray of freshly baked biscuits.

"Hi, Grandma Eloise!" Anna said, running over and giving her a hug. Madeline was surprised that her mother had continued to allow Anna to call her grandma, and then she realized that if she ever married Brady, Eloise could kind of be a grandma figure to Anna.

"Well, hello, Anna." Eloise said, setting down the tray and hugging her back. "I'm so glad that you could come today. I hope you enjoy all this great food."

"Me, too. I love Thanksgiving." Anna said. Anna was always filled with excitement about everything. It was impressive to Madeline, given the background and upbringing that she'd had for so many years.

"Everything looks just wonderful, Madeline. Thank you for inviting us," Jasmine said.

"Of course, Thanksgiving is about family, and you're family," Madeline said, giving her a hug. Jasmine had done such a good job at being Madeline's assistant, and they had become so much closer in the last few months. Brady was talking with Geneva and Clemmy, but then walked over to Madeline and wrapped his arms around her from behind.

"You've done an incredible job, sweetie. Everything looks perfect today." Madeline turned and looked up at him, putting her hand on his cheek.

"It's perfect because all of you are here. That's what makes this Thanksgiving the most special one I've ever had." As she said it to him, a part of her wanted to laugh. It sounded like some cheesy line out of a romance novel. She'd written those lines many times in her career, and now she was actually living it.

As everyone mingled, chatted, and laughed in the warm space, Madeline felt a sense of contentment wash over her. This was her family, her community, and she was so thankful for every person in the room. She looked around at the faces of these people that she loved, these people that loved her and accepted her, and she knew this was going to be a Thanksgiving to remember. It would be a time to celebrate new traditions, to reconnect relationships, and just enjoy being together.

Madeline had set the table with a rustic elegance that really captured the essence of fall. In the middle sat the golden turkey which had been cooked to perfection. It was surrounded by a variety of other dishes including roast beef, mashed potatoes with gravy, dressing that had been baked in a casserole dish just like her grandmother had cooked, a giant salad, and green beans. There were also candied yams and all kinds of other dishes on the table. They could barely fit their own dinner plates there was so much food. Madeline worried a bit about how many leftovers she was going to end up with. She would definitely be sending them home with everyone.

The smell of the feast filled the room, blending in with the scent of the pumpkin and coffee-scented candles and the smell of a crackling fireplace. Madeline stood at the head of the table, a smile on her face.

"Everybody, please take a seat. I'm so excited that you're all here," she said. Brady sat next to Madeline with Eloise on his other side. Geneva, who was at the other end of the table, sat next to Eloise, and then Jasmine, Anna, and finally Clemmy. "Before we dig into all this food, I just want to say how thankful that I am for each of you." She looked at each person individually. "This year has been a crazy year of change for me. I've had challenges. Some of you have been witness to that at times, but I couldn't be more thankful to share this moment with all of you."

Brady reached over and squeezed her hand before she sat down.

"Would anyone like to say grace?" Geneva asked, looking around the table.

"I'd be honored," Clemmy said. She bowed her head, and everyone followed suit. "Dear Lord, thank you for this food and for the loving hands that prepared it. Thank you for family, both the one that we're born into and the one that we have chosen. Please protect everyone this holiday season and let us enjoy this amazing meal. Amen."

Everyone echoed “amen” in unison.

As they began to eat and plates were passed around, there was a symphony of oohs and ahs that filled the room as everyone took their first bites.

"Madeline, this turkey is amazing,” Geneva said.

"Thank you. It's my first turkey, so I was a little worried,” Madeline admitted.

"And these mashed potatoes are just heavenly,” Jasmine added. Anna, who had been eagerly taking bites of everything she could reach, finally spoke up.

"This is all so yummy. Can we eat like this every day?" Laughter erupted around the table.

"If we did, we would all need to join a gym by New Year’s,” Eloise said, laughing. Brady looked at Anna.

"So have you decided what you want for Christmas, little girl?" Her eyes sparkled.

"Yeah, I want a telescope. I've been learning about stars and planets at school, and I want to see them up close for myself."

"That's a great idea,” Eloise said, "The universe is full of wonders that are waiting to be discovered."

Madeline was happy to see her mother fully engaging in the moment. Since she'd never had her own children, she hadn't seen her mother exhibit that grandmotherly charm before, but she was definitely doing that now.

"So, speaking of Christmas," Madeline said, "Brady and I are going to cut down our own tree tomorrow, and then we'll spend the day decorating the cabin."

"You're going to cut down your own tree?" Eloise said, surprised. "That doesn't sound like the Madeline I knew. She was all about pre-lit Christmas trees that came in a box." Brady stared at Madeline, his mouth hanging open.

"I'm going to pretend I don't know that about you."

Madeline waved her hand. "I was a different person back then. That was before I even owned a pair of hiking boots or knew every kind of mushroom in the forest." She cut her eyes over at Geneva.

"Listen, I like to teach you things, whether you want to learn them or not."

"Well, I think cutting down your own tree sounds great," Clemmy said. "There's just nothing like the scent of a fresh cut tree to bring in that Christmas spirit."

"Absolutely, and don't forget the Christmas parade and festival are coming up. It's just going to be the most magical season," Geneva said.

The meal continued with the conversation flowing naturally. They talked a bit about Clemmy's son who was stationed overseas and how much she missed him. Geneva talked about some of her upcoming nature hikes after the first of the year. Jasmine talked a little bit about working for Madeline and how she was really enjoying learning marketing. She said she might even branch out at some point by taking other clients. Even Eloise piped in a time or two about her thoughts on Jubilee, almost all of them positive.

Finally, as they took their last bites of food and everyone leaned back full and content, Madeline felt a great sense of accomplishment. Her first Thanksgiving dinner had been a resounding success, but more importantly, she had gotten to spend it with the people that she loved the most in the world.

"Can I ask everybody to do something?" she asked as they were all sitting in their turkey comas.

"Of course. What is it?" Brady asked.

"Well, I know we probably should have done this before we started dinner, but this is my first time hosting Thanksgiving, so you have to cut me some slack. Anyway, I was wondering if everybody could go around the table and say what they're most thankful for this year."

"That sounds like a great idea," Geneva said. "I'll start. I'm thankful for my brand new neighbor and friend, Madeline."

"Oh, Geneva. That's so sweet. But you have to be thankful for something else."

"Nope, that's it for me this year," she said smiling and leaning back with her hand on her stomach. "I'm also thankful for stretch pants."

"What about you, Clemmy?"

She thought for a moment. "I'm thankful that I get to do what I love every day and be surrounded by books and wonderful customers."

"That's a good one," Madeline said. "What about you, Jasmine?"

"I'm thankful for new beginnings." Her eyes welled with tears a bit. Madeline didn't press further because she knew exactly what Jasmine meant.

"Okay. What about you, Anna?"

"Well, I'm thankful for my horse, and my Uncle Brady, and I'm thankful for my new friends at school."

"Those are really great things," Eloise said, reaching over and patting her hand.

"Okay, Mom, what about you?"

Eloise thought for a moment. "I agree with Jasmine; I'm grateful for new beginnings and forgiveness. What about you, my daughter?" Madeline smiled.

"Ditto. I am also thankful for a second chance at love and a first chance at having a community around me." She looked over at Brady, who was smiling at each of them.

"I guess it's my turn," he said, reaching over and taking her hand. "I'm thankful that God brought the love of my life here to Jubilee, even if he had to do it while she was kicking and screaming."

Everybody laughed, and Madeline knew she was exactly where she needed to be. Jubilee was home, but more than that, these people were her home.

It was a cold, crisp day, and as they stepped out of the car, the scent of pine overwhelmed Madeline's senses. When they pulled into the Christmas tree farm, she was shocked because she had never seen so many Christmas trees lined up one-by-one. Sure, she had seen Christmas tree lots back in the city where the trees were already cut down and you just simply walked up and picked one. She didn't even go that far. She bought one in a store that was in a box and snapped together really quickly, and then she would light a pine scented candle. That was about the extent of her Christmas decorations. Here there were rows upon rows of evergreen trees stretched out before her, like a sea of potential Christmas cheer. Brady parked the truck and turned off the engine.

"So are we ready to go find the perfect tree?" he asked, his voice filled with boy-like excitement.

"Absolutely," Madeline said, excited for this new thing she got to do with Brady. Anna had already unbuckled her seatbelt and was about to burst out of the truck, her eyes wide with wonder. It dawned on Madeline that she had probably never seen anything like this either. Her young life had been marred by an abusive father and a dysfunctional situation. It was highly doubtful that she'd ever seen a Christmas tree farm before.

"Look at all of these trees. Can we get the biggest one?" Anna asked. Brady laughed as he stepped out and helped Madeline down.

"Well, it has to fit in the cabin, but we'll try to get the biggest one we can. I promise."

They made their way down into the farm, each

step crunching leaves on the frosty ground below. This farm was a local favorite. It had been family-owned for generations. A few other people were also there, laughter and chatter filling the air. Madeline felt peaceful. This place was beautiful, just like every other place in Jubilee. But this would be the first time she had ever participated in cutting down her own Christmas tree, and she didn't know exactly what was required of her. Most likely, it would be Brady, with his big muscular arms, taking care of getting the tree to the ground. She loved the authenticity of this experience and sharing it with the people that she loved. Anna ran up ahead, her eyes darting from tree to tree.

"What about this one?" she called, pointing to a tall, somewhat sparse tree. Before Brady could answer, she found a different one that was even better. Finally, she settled on one, and Brady walked over to examine it.

"Hmm... This is a bit thin, don't you think?" Anna's eyes narrowed as she looked at him, putting her little hands on her hips.

"Okay, Mr. Tree Expert, then you pick one." Madeline laughed at their easy banter. Brady winked at her and then turned his attention to a robust Fraser fir a few feet away.

"How about this one? It has these big full branches, and it seems to be just the right height for Madeline's cabin." Madeline walked over, her fingers gently touching the needles.

"It's beautiful, but don't you want to get one for the trailer too?" Brady shook his head.

"We're going to get a small little tree from the store and some other decorations but, if you don't mind, we plan on spending a lot of our Christmas season at the cabin."

"I will love having all of you around for the holidays, so feel free to take my cabin over," Madeline said, rubbing his arm.

He smiled. "All right, we have to make sure that this is the right height." Brady pulled a tape measure from his pocket and stretched it. After a few quick measurements, he nodded. "Okay. It's perfect."

Anna clapped her hands and jumped up and down. "Yay. Let's cut it down."

Brady took a saw from a nearby shed, and with Anna's eager assistance, they each took turns cutting. Eventually, the tree finally gave way with a soft thud, hitting the ground. They picked it up and loaded it into the truck bed, securing it with ropes before paying the attendant. Madeline was so excited that this tree would be the centerpiece of her first country Christmas. It would be a symbol of the new traditions and memories she would make in Jubilee.

They climbed back into the truck, and Anna nestled between them.

"Hot cocoa when we get home?" Brady suggested as he started the engine. Madeline leaned in, giving him a quick kiss.

"Hot cocoa sounds perfect."

"Y'all are really gross," Anna said, rolling her eyes and crossing her arms.

As they drove off from the tree farm, the rows of trees growing smaller in the rear-view mirror, Madeline felt a warmth spread through her. This was the magic of the season, she realized. All the other Christmases she had ever experienced paled in comparison to this one, and it wasn't even Christmas yet.

CHAPTER 11

They got the Christmas tree back to Madeline's cabin and brought it inside. While Brady was working on getting it set up, the cabin was filled with the comforting aroma of hot chocolate, cinnamon, and of course, the fresh scent of pine from the newly erected Christmas tree.

Madeline turned on a playlist of classic Christmas songs, which hummed softly from the speaker she had hidden behind the TV. It filled the room with a sense of holiday joy and nostalgia.

She lit the fireplace because it was so cold outside today. It made the perfect setting for decorating the cabin. Jasmine had some things that she wanted to get done in town, mainly Christmas shopping without her daughter around, so it was just Madeline, Brady, Anna, and Eloise in the cabin.

Brady was on his knees, his brow furrowed in concentration as he tried to untangle a stubborn knot in a string of white lights. His flannel shirt was rolled up at the sleeves, which revealed his strong forearms, as he made quick work of the tangle.

Anna was tasked with carefully laying out the brand new Christmas ornaments that Madeline had purchased for the cabin. She'd had such a fun time shopping online and in local shops, looking for the most rustic Christmas ornaments. She had bears and pine cones and all kinds of other things that were going to look beautiful on the tree and really make the cabin feel like a cozy place for Christmas.

She also had some hand-painted glass ornaments and a few rustic wooden pieces that Brady had brought over from his family collection. Although he had lost most everything in the fire, he did have a few boxes of keepsakes that were stored in the barn, up in the loft. He was thankful when he found them recently.

Anna was practically vibrating with excitement. It made Madeline so happy to see that. After all the stuff that Anna and Jasmine had been through in their lives, it was a wonderful thing to see them enjoying a holiday season without stress.

Anna danced and sang to the Christmas songs, at

least the ones that she knew, her eyes wide and sparkling. She alternated between sorting through the ornaments and running over to Brady to see what he was doing.

Eloise had laid down to take a nap, but finally came out into the living room to see what everyone was doing. She drank a cup of hot cocoa, topped with a generous dollop of whipped cream, as she watched them.

"All right, team," Madeline said, clapping her hands together, "our mission, should we all choose to accept it, is to transform this tree into a Christmas masterpiece."

Anna squealed with delight and ran over to the box of ornaments again. "I get to put the star on the top, right?"

"We're going to save that special moment for last," Brady said. "Why don't you just start with these ornaments? You can be our person who puts the ornaments on the low part of the tree, since Madeline and I are too old to bend down that far."

Madeline punched him in the arm playfully. Anna hung the first ornament, and as she did, Eloise started to reminisce.

"Madeline, when you were Anna's age, you were so determined when it came to decorating the

Christmas tree. You would stand on your tiptoes, stretching as high as you could, just to put ornaments in the perfect spot."

Madeline chuckled, "Well, I guess some things never change."

"You're right, they don't," Eloise said. "But I wouldn't have had it any other way. Those were some of those times that you were truly, utterly happy as a child. A mother always wants to remember those."

Brady stopped hanging the ornaments for just a moment to join the conversation. "You know, Christmas at the farm was different, but it was special in its own way. We would always chop down our own tree from the backwoods. My grandparents would share stories from Christmases of their youth, about the harsh winters and humble gifts, but always about the love. We would sit around the fireplace and just feel grateful at the simple joy of being together. We even roasted marshmallows a time or two."

Anna's eyes lit up again. "Can we do that today?"

Brady put up his hand, "Why don't we save that for another day? We've got a lot going on. I'll build you a big bonfire at the farm soon, and we'll roast all the marshmallows you want."

"Your Christmases sound wonderfully heart-warming, Brady," Madeline said.

"They were. The farm is a lot smaller now. My grandparents sold off some land many years ago before I inherited it, but it's still home and it's still filled with love."

"Do you think Santa is going to bring me that unicorn doll I asked for?" Anna suddenly asked. Much like many children, she was all over the place with her topics.

"Well, if you've been a good girl, I'm sure he will," Eloise said.

The time had come to put on the tree's crowning glory, the star.

"It's your moment, Anna," Brady announced. He lifted her up onto his broad shoulders, steadying her as she reached the top to place the bright gold star at the pinnacle of the tree.

"I did it!" Anna yelled, grinning from ear to ear.

Everybody stepped back to admire their handiwork. The room was now bathed in a magical glow from the Christmas lights, each of them twinkling off of the different Christmas ornaments Madeline had purchased. She almost wanted to shed a few tears as she thought about the many years to come that she would get to see these same ornaments on the tree. Hopefully, there would be lots of memories between now and then.

Maybe one day they would stand around it as a married couple. Maybe they would stand there when Anna graduated from high school or when she got married someday. Madeline realized she was putting a lot of thought into this, given that she had just started dating Brady a few months ago.

"To family, new traditions and the magic of Christmas," Eloise suddenly said, standing up and raising her mug of hot chocolate.

"And to love, friendship, and the joy of being with the people you care most about in the world," Madeline added.

They each clinked their mug of hot chocolate together, took a sip and then stood there in silence as they looked at the tree, the crackling sound of the fireplace off in the distance. As the evening went on, Anna got tired and her eyes grew heavy with sleep. Eloise took her into the guest bedroom where they snuggled up to watch a Christmas movie.

Soon Madeline looked in the door and saw that Anna and Eloise were both fast asleep. Anna's dreams were probably filled with Christmas trees and unicorns. Left alone in the living room, Madeline and Brady settled into the plush sofa in front of the fireplace. The room was lit up with the soft light of the fire and the twinkling of the Christmas tree beside them.

"I think this must be the most perfect moment in my life," Madeline whispered, leaning into his embrace.

"It's more than perfect," he said, his arm wrapping around her. "You have turned this cabin into a home, Madeline Harper. I'm just incredibly grateful that you allowed me and my family to be a part of it."

She looked at him and stole a quick kiss. As they sat in front of the warmth of the fire, Madeline now understood what people meant when they talked about the peace of Christmas.

The atmosphere at the only bookstore in Jubilee was electric. There was a line of readers snaked around all the shelves, each of them holding one of Madeline's books.

She was always so excited to meet her readers. It was one of her favorite parts of being an author. She could smell the freshly brewed coffee and asked Jasmine to bring her a cup before the signing started. Above the table where Madeline sat hung a banner that said *Meet Bestselling Author Madeline Harper Today*. She looked up and saw her mother from across the room and waved her over. It looked like Eloise was just trying to stay out of the way, but Madeline wanted her to be a part of what was going on so she could finally see what her author life was like.

"Did you need something, dear?" Eloise asked as she walked over.

"No, I just thought maybe you might like to sit with me while I sign some books."

"Oh, I don't want to get in the way."

"Mom, you're not getting in the way. Just sit down and take a load off." Eloise sat down next to her and rested her hands atop each other on the table in front of her.

"Okay, but don't ask me to make any speeches."

"Don't worry. I don't plan to."

"Are you ready?" Clemmy asked.

"Yes. You can start sending readers over," Madeline said, looking up at her and smiling. The first reader walked over with a huge grin on her face and slid one of Madeline's older books in front of her.

"Hi, Madeline. It is so nice to meet you! I've been so excited about this."

“It’s great to meet you! What's your name?" Madeline asked.

“Carol.”

"Well, it's good to meet you, Carol. Would you like me to personalize the book?"

"Yes, please."

As she signed it and made more small talk, her mother looked on. Madeline didn't dare look directly at her because she wasn't sure if she was going to say something critical, or if she was actually enjoying the moment. Several other readers came up, had their books signed and had their pictures taken with Madeline. The whole time, Eloise just sat and smiled as she watched her daughter do her thing. Finally, an older woman walked up and set a book in front of Madeline.

"Hi, Madeline. It’s so good to meet you. My name is Denise, and I just wanted to tell you that your books got me through my chemo treatments." Madeline had heard that many times in her career. People taking chemo treatments often needed something to do to pass the time, and she had gotten so many letters over the years from people thanking her for her books. "The stories that you craft, well, they gave me something to look forward to. They made me believe in happy endings again." The woman had tears in her eyes. Madeline stood up and gave her a hug, took a picture with her, and then signed her book. As she walked away, Madeline looked over at her mother who was wiping a stray tear from her own eye.

The signing continued as more readers came up to the table. The afternoon wore on, and Madeline met fans who had driven for hours just to see her. That always amazed her that people would come from that far. A young couple even told her that one of her books had inspired their own love story, and another reader said that she was working on writing her first book because Madeline had encouraged her.

There were so many stories of people who said that Madeline's books had touched them. One woman had lost her husband of over forty years and had stopped loving to read, but Madeline's books had brought her back into it. Another woman said that she and her sister used to share their love of reading, and when her sister had passed away, the only thing that she had to keep honoring her memory was to read. She'd found Madeline's books and had been able to continue her love of reading. The stories went on and on, and Madeline watched as her mother became more and more invested in them.

When it was finally over and they said their goodbyes, Madeline and Eloise walked outside to her car.

"Madeline, can I say something?" Eloise asked before they got to the car. Madeline stopped.

"Of course, Mom."

"I heard what all of those readers were saying about you, and I just want to say that I'm sorry for all the snide comments I've made about you being a romance author over the years. I never understood how much your writing has meant to people, how much it has helped them, and it's certainly more than I've ever done with my life to help people."

Madeline reached out and put her hand on her mother's arm. "Don't say that. You've done things to help people."

"Not like you, my dear daughter. I am eternally sorry for the things I've said. I think sometimes from my own pain, I lashed out."

"It has always been more than just a job to me, and I'm glad that you can see that now. I feel like it's my calling, my way to connect and offer comfort and hope to people when they need it most."

"I have been dismissive of your work, your passion, for many years, and I now see how wrong I was. Your writing has changed people's lives, and I just want you to know that I couldn't be prouder of you."

Madeline was too choked up to speak. When she finally found her voice again, all she could say was, "Thank you, Mom. That means more to me than you'll ever know."

The Rustic Spoon was buzzing with the lunchtime crowd, and the air was filled with the aroma of hearty winter stews and freshly baked bread. Madeline sat with Clemmy at a corner table, the cozy spot decorated for Christmas. The atmosphere in the diner was always rustic and warm, making it feel like it was an extension of someone's home.

"I just can't believe it, Clemmy. My mom actually said that she was proud of me, that she was proud of my writing and how I've helped people. Do you know how long I've waited to hear those words?"

Clemmy looked up from her chicken Caesar salad. "That's wonderful, Madeline. You've worked so hard to mend your relationship. I remember how you were worried this wasn't going to work out when your mother first got here, but you really hung in there, and you deserve that praise."

Just as Madeline was about to respond, her phone buzzed on the table, interrupting the moment. She looked down at the screen, puzzled. "It's an unknown number. Maybe I shouldn't answer it. It's usually a scammer."

"Well, you never know. Go ahead and take it."

Madeline answered the call. "Hello?"

"Madeline, dear, I'm so glad I caught you. This is Hilda from Willow Creek Estates where your mother lives. I hope I'm not intruding, but I've been quite worried. She hasn't been home in a long time and she's not answering her phone."

"Oh, she's here with me in Jubilee, up in the mountains. She's been visiting with me for a while now."

"What a relief," Hilda said, sighing. "I'm so glad she found a doctor closer to you to do her knee surgery. She's been talking about it and worrying over it for months."

Madeline felt like the floor had dropped from underneath her. "Knee surgery? She hasn't mentioned anything to me about knee surgery."

Hilda paused for a long moment, sensing

tension. "Oh, dear. I thought you knew. I'm so sorry, Madeline."

"It's okay. Thank you for letting me know," Madeline said, her voice barely above a whisper. She pressed end and sat there staring at her phone, feeling a mixture of confusion and betrayal.

Clemmy could see that something was wrong and reached across the table to touch her hand. "What happened? You look like you've seen a ghost."

"My mom didn't come here to mend our relationship, Clemmy. She came here because she apparently needs knee surgery and wanted someone to take care of her. Of course, she never told me that."

Clemmy's eyes widened, her mouth forming a silent "oh."

"I feel so foolish," Madeline said. "Here I was, thinking we were finally on the path to a better relationship, and it turns out she had an ulterior motive all along."

"I'm so sorry. I know this is a tough pill to swallow. But maybe this is some kind of sign that the universe is giving you both a second chance, even if the circumstance isn't what you thought."

"I don't know, Clemmy. I feel so deceived. I mean, how do I even confront her about this?"

"Very carefully. Don't let this setback erase all the

progress that you've made. Sometimes life throws these curveballs to test us, to see if we're really ready for the change that we've been seeking."

Madeline took a deep breath. "You're right. I know I need to talk to her. I need to find out the whole story, but I'm not ready yet."

Clemmy nodded. "And whatever happens, you're not alone. You've got all of us, people who love you and support you no matter what."

"Thank you. I don't know what I would do without you." As they returned to their meal, Madeline felt like she'd lost her appetite. She couldn't shake the feeling of betrayal and uncertainty that was clouding her thoughts. She knew that she might need a few days before she said something to her mother. She needed to think through her words carefully before she ruined any chance at them having a relationship.

CHAPTER 12

Frannie sat outside at one of her new bistro tables, trying to take a break and savor a rare moment of stillness. Her bakery was opening tomorrow, and every time she thought about it, she got butterflies in her stomach and her heart raced to levels that she hadn't felt before.

Her clipboard was resting beside her, filled with all the last minute to-dos for tomorrow's grand opening. Whisk Me Away was the name she had chosen after finding her grandmother's prized whisk in the drawer at her house. She'd had a charming sign created, and now it hung above the bakery's entrance.

Just as she was about to dive back into her checklist of things that she needed to get done, she heard the familiar jingle of dog tags. She looked up to see

Lanelle, the owner of All Tucked Inn, approaching with Murphy, the town's honorary, four-legged mayor, who sat in the window at the top of the Inn and overlooked his beloved town. He was happily trotting beside her on a leash.

"Frannie, darling, you look like you could use a break," Lanelle called out. She walked over and stood beside the table. Frannie smiled. She loved Lanelle, but she loved Murphy the most. She'd only seen him in pictures from her Nana, so she was excited to finally meet him in person. She reached down and scratched the top of his head.

"What a wonderful surprise. Please have a seat."

Lanelle took the chair across from Frannie while Murphy settled at their feet, his tail wagging for a bit before he passed out onto the sidewalk. "This place is shaping up beautifully," Lanelle said, looking up at the sign. "And I love the name, Whisk Me Away. That is just too adorable."

Frannie felt proud. "Thank you. I wanted it to be a tribute to Nana, as well as a reflection of the experience I hope people have here. I want them to be whisked away by the delicious treats they'll have and forget all the problems in the real world."

"Your grandmother would've been so proud,

Frannie. You know, I knew her for a very long time. We were in the same Sunday School class as kids."

"Thank you. I hope she would've been proud."

"So, besides coming over here to wish you the best for tomorrow and let you know that I'm going to come over and eat my weight in cupcakes, I did have another reason for stopping by. How would you feel about supplying some of your pastries to the inn? Our guests would love to have some local flavors, and it might be a great way to introduce your bakery to a wider audience. You know, we do a wonderful continental breakfast."

Frannie's eyes widened. "Lanelle, that would be incredible. I'd be absolutely honored to do that."

Lanelle clapped her hands together. "Oh, I'm thrilled. Just imagine breakfast at All Tucked Inn featuring pastries from Whisk Me Away. We'll be famous in no time!" she said, laughing. Murphy barked approvingly as if he was the one to seal the deal as mayor.

"Thank you. You know, this journey to opening the bakery has been quite a rollercoaster of highs and lows. Leaving my career behind wasn't something that was easy for me either, but it's moments like this and support like yours that make it all worthwhile. Coming back to this community that felt like home is really a blessing to me."

Lanelle smiled. “You're going to do great things, my dear. Jubilee is lucky to have you back."

As Lanelle and Murphy walked away, Murphy turning back one more time to bark, Frannie sat there a moment longer. Her heart was full. The sun was setting, casting its farewell glow on the mountains beyond. Tomorrow was a big day, filled with some unknowns, but she felt like she was exactly where she needed to be and her grandmother was watching over her.

Madeline stormed into her home office, her emotions getting the better of her. As she flung the door open, it almost flew off the hinges. She needed to distance herself from her mother because just the drive home had gotten her all worked up again as she thought about it. As she entered, she found Jasmine hunched over the laptop, diligently working on social media updates.

"Hey, Madeline," Jasmine said in her normal peppy tone, "How did the..."

Madeline cut her off, "Can you believe this? Can

you believe this? My mother came to Jubilee not to mend our relationship like she said, but because she apparently needs knee surgery and wanted somebody to take care of her. She never even told me this. I had to find it out from some random lady that lives in her retirement community."

Jasmine's eyes were wide as she took in the information. She slowly closed her laptop, giving Madeline her full attention. "Oh, wow. That's a lot of information to take in."

Madeline sank into her plush office chair, her hands shaking, as she tried to make some sense of her feelings. "You know, I have been bending over backward trying to make her feel comfortable here, trying to mend fences, and all this time she had an ulterior motive. I mean, when was she going to tell me? The day of her surgery?"

Jasmine rolled her chair closer to Madeline's desk, her eyes filled with concern. "That's really tough, Madeline. Maybe she was afraid to tell you, or maybe she thought you'd say no."

Madeline sighed. "That's just it, Jasmine. I would've said yes. I'm her only child. Despite everything she's done, she's still my mother. But now I feel so deceived, like all of this has just been a ruse, like she's just been playing some big joke on me this entire time."

"I get it. Trust is a very fragile thing and once it's broken, it's hard to rebuild. But, I've been around you and your mom, and I don't think she's been pretending. I can see the genuine love for you in her eyes. I think she just lost her way, and once she hadn't told you for so long, she didn't know how to tell you at all."

“What do I do now? How do I confront her without blowing up?"

Jasmine leaned back like she was choosing her words carefully. "Well, first you need to know that you have every right to be upset, but maybe you have to approach this from a place of trying to understand her, rather than accusing her. Ask her why she felt like she couldn't be honest with you. Sometimes the why can explain a lot of the what."

"I know you're right. I need to know why she did this. Maybe then we can somehow figure out a way to move forward, if that's even possible. But right now, I'm still so emotionally raw that I don't think it's a good time to have this conversation with her."

"Whatever happens, you're not alone, okay? You can always vent to me and Brady. He can't get away from you. You're his girlfriend."

Madeline laughed. "Thank you, Jasmine. I don't

know what I would do without all of you. I swear I feel like everybody in Jubilee is going to end up becoming my therapist before it's over with."

"That's what families are for, Madeline. To lift each other up, especially when other people let us down. That's what you did for me and my daughter, and I'll always be here to do that for you."

Madeline stood up. "All right, we've got to get back to work. I've got a new book to outline and editing to do. I can't give in to all of these crazy emotions right now."

"Well, if you have some time, I'd like to show you some new social media posts I've created."

"That would be a welcome distraction."

The air was thick with anticipation as Frannie stood at the door of her brand new bakery. She flipped the sign to show that it was open and unlocked the door, welcoming the townspeople of Jubilee to come inside. She took in a deep breath, which was mainly filled with the scents of cinnamon, vanilla, and freshly brewed coffee. Today was the day that her dream and her grandmother's dream would finally become a reality.

She pushed open the glass door, the little bell chimed, and people started flowing in. She had hired a couple of high school kids to help her until she could get some permanent employees. She wanted to be able to walk around and greet people, but have people running the cash register at the same time.

It was a cozy, yet vibrant atmosphere that she'd created. Perky's grandson was playing guitar over in the corner, a selection of Christmas songs they had chosen together. Rustic wooden tables were scattered around the room, each one holding a vase of poinsettias. The chandelier overhead cast a warm, inviting glow, making the beautiful wood floors gleam.

The focal point of the bakery was the long dessert counter, marble topped, and showcasing everything that Frannie had made in anticipation for the opening. Trays of Lula's Lemon Bars, chocolate chip cookies as big as your hand, and gooey melt-in-your-mouth pieces of cake in every flavor adorned the long counter. There were scones in a variety of flavors, from plain ones to cranberry-orange, and a three-tiered cake stand showed off an abundance of cupcakes, each one a miniature work of art. Swirls of buttercream frosting in shades of pink, blue, and lavender were on display. Then there were the pies - apple, cherry, and Nana Lula's famous pecan-chocolate pie. Each pie had its own golden, flaky, buttery crust.

The crowd was a mixture of familiar faces and tourists who were in town to look at the mountains for the holiday season. They had all been drawn in by the buzz that had been building for a few weeks now. Geneva was there talking with Perky, and Frannie finally got to meet Madeline, as well as her mother, Eloise, who was visiting town. Everybody was shoving pastries in their faces at an alarming rate, which made Frannie giggle. Apparently, the town had really needed some place to get sugary goodness all these years. Brady and Jasmine came with Jasmine's little girl, her eyes wide with wonder as she looked at all the desserts.

The atmosphere was exactly what Frannie had wanted. It was electric, a blend of excitement and community spirit. Every now and then, Frannie would hear people speaking words of praise, about their plans to return, and some people were even making requests for holiday orders. And then, as she stood there taking it all in, she suddenly saw Cole across the room. He was leaning against a wall, handsome as ever, a proud smile on his face.

"You did it," he mouthed to her. In that moment, Frannie almost burst into tears. She was so thankful to have this new chance. Not only a new chance at a career that she would love, but at the love she thought she'd lost years ago.

The sun was starting to set earlier these days as the winter settled in over Jubilee. There was a light dusting of snow on the mountaintops today, and the air was crisp but not yet biting. It was all a reminder that December had arrived in Jubilee.

Today, Madeline was taking a trail ride with Brady, trying to get her mind off the situation with her mother. She didn't want to approach it the wrong way and ruin any chance at a relationship. As much as she was mad at her mother, she also had enjoyed spending time with her cooking Thanksgiving dinner and decorating the Christmas tree. She wondered if it was all an act, but a part of her knew that it wasn't. Her mother wasn't that good of an actress.

She felt the rhythmic motion of the horse beneath her, a comforting sway that was usually good at putting her at ease. But today, her thoughts were all over the place. Each one trying to get her attention.

Brady rode along beside her quietly, his posture relaxed, but his eyes showing concern. His horse seemed to pick up on his mood, treading more gently along the winding narrow trail. After what felt like a long time of silence, Brady finally spoke. "Madeline, you've been really quiet. Is there something on your mind you want to talk about?"

She sighed. “It's my mom, Brady. I asked Jasmine not to tell you until I got a chance to, but I found out she's been keeping something from me, something big, and I just don't know what to do about it."

Brady stopped his horse and looked at her. "Do you want to share what it is?"

"I got a phone call from a woman who lives in the same community as her. I guess they're friends. It turns out that she needs knee surgery, and that's why she came to Jubilee. She didn't have anybody to take care of her, so she didn't really come to rebuild our relationship. She came because she needed a caregiver after her surgery."

Brady exhaled deeply, his breath visible in the cool air. "Wow. That's shocking, Madeline. And it's heavy. Really heavy."

"I know. And the worst part is she hasn't said

anything about it. I had to find out from a perfect stranger. I don't know why she didn't trust me with this. I mean, when was she planning on telling me? Was she just going to call me from the hospital one day and say, 'Hey, pick me up.'"

Brady shook his head. "This is a tough pill to swallow, I know. I can't imagine how betrayed you must feel."

Madeline's eyes were welling with tears, but she blinked them back. The last thing she needed to do was fall off a horse on top of everything else. "I do feel betrayed. It makes it even worse that we were making such good progress. I thought we were finally in a place where we could have a real mother-daughter relationship and where we could be honest with each other. I let my guard down."

"I know this is hard, Madeline, but this is a good opportunity for you to have a real honest conversation with your mom. It's clear that she needs you, even if she's not willing to admit it."

"I want to have a conversation. I do. But how can I have an honest conversation with a woman who has lied to me like this?"

"Sometimes people keep secrets because they're scared, Madeline. Afraid of judgment, afraid of rejection. Maybe your mom thought if she told you why she was here, that you would send her packing because you hadn't spoken in so many years. I'm sure showing up on your front porch was scary for her."

"You're giving her a lot of credit, Brady."

He chuckled under his breath. "I'm giving her the benefit of the doubt because sometimes that's what we have to do with family, even when it's hard."

They started riding again and continued until they reached a clearing overlooking a small pond. The water was still reflecting the twilight sky and the snow-capped mountains in the distance. Brady jumped off and helped Madeline down from her horse. They tied them to a tree and sat on a fallen log.

“So, you think I’m overreacting?”

"Look, I can't tell you how to feel or what to do about your mom, but I can tell you that holding on to resentment and anger is only going to hurt you in the long run. I just went through this with Jasmine. You know how upset I was with her at the beginning, but we've worked through it, and that is hard work. It's not easy to forgive someone or forgive yourself, for that matter. It's not easy to let people back in your life that haven't been there in a long time."

"I know you're right. It's just so hard to let go of the anger."

He moved closer, putting his arm around her. "You don't have to do it alone. Whatever you decide, I'll always be right here beside you."

"Thank you. That means more to me than you could ever know."

"And for what it's worth, I think this is going to work itself out. I think you'll have a good conversation with your mom and get all of this squared away, and then you'll have a really solid relationship."

"You're always so positive, Brady Nolan."

As she leaned into his embrace, Madeline felt a sense of peace wash over her. That's the way she always felt when she was in Brady's arms.

CHAPTER 13

Madeline sat at the dining room table pushing food around on her plate with her fork and staring out mindlessly at the mountains. The aroma of barbecue chicken and garlic mashed potatoes wafted through the air, but she'd lost her appetite.

Her mother sat across from her, quietly enjoying her meal, seemingly unaware of the tension that was hanging in the air above the table. Finally, Eloise looked up, her eyes meeting Madeline's.

"Is something wrong, dear? You've hardly eaten your food, and you've been awfully quiet."

Madeline took a deep breath, her heart pounding like a jackhammer inside her chest. "Mom, we need to talk about something. I should have talked to you about it a few days ago when I first found out, but I needed some time to deal with it."

Eloise set her fork down, her eyes narrowing with concern. "This sounds serious. What's going on?"

Madeline hesitated. Her fingers gripping her fork like it was some sort of weapon. "Why didn't you tell me you're planning to have knee surgery here in Jubilee?"

Eloise's mouth dropped open, and her eyes widened. Her face turned pale in an instant. "How did you..."

"I got a call from Hilda, your neighbor. She was worried because you haven't been in touch or answering your phone. She mentioned the surgery."

Eloise's shoulders slumped. "Hilda. That old busybody. I was going to tell you, Madeline, I swear I was. I just didn't know how."

Madeline felt the anger starting to rise within her again. "You didn't know how? Mom, you've been here for weeks, and you didn't once think to mention that you needed to have surgery, that you actually came here so that I could take care of you and not because you really wanted to mend our relationship?"

Eloise looked down, her eyes filling with regret.

"I was very afraid, Madeline. I was afraid if I told you that when I got here, you would send me back home if you knew the real reason I came. And once I was here, I realized that I did want to mend our relationship, that there was a chance we could be mother and daughter again."

"But that doesn't change the fact that you came here under false pretenses. And let me think that I was so important to you that you came all the way here just to fix our relationship. I put up with all the things that you said, all the criticisms, because I thought we were working toward something. But instead, all you were doing was angling for a caregiver."

"I am so sorry, Madeline. Once I was here, things really started changing between us, and then I was too scared to tell you about the surgery."

"So you thought lying to me was a better option? Deceiving me? You know, you've spent years being critical of me, Mom, but you never lied to me. That was never the issue between us. I don't know if I can ever trust you."

"I didn't lie, darling. I've wanted to work on our relationship for years. This knee thing gave me a reason to see you. And yes, I also came here because I need the surgery. I found out about six months ago, and I do need somebody to help me recover. You're my only family. I thought maybe if I came and worked on the relationship that it would be natural for me to tell you about the surgery. But then we were having such a good time that I didn't want to ruin anything."

"You could have been honest with me, Mom. After all these years, after all the distance between us, you could have taken this opportunity to be honest with me."

Eloise reached across the table, her hand trembling as she touched Madeline's. "You're right. I should have been honest. I let my fear get the best of me. And I'm truly sorry. And I'll understand if you want me to go home. I can hire help to come sit with me after surgery."

"You know I'm not going to let you go home and have surgery alone," Madeline said, putting her fork down. "But why now? Why decide to have the surgery now?"

"I've been putting it off for years. I've been in pain, but it's become unbearable. The doctor has been giving me injections in my knee. I can't go on like this."

"I would've been there for you. You didn't have to

go through this alone. You didn't have to delay your surgery."

"I guess I wasn't sure how I would be received if I asked you to take care of me after being apart for so many years. It's not lost on me that I've been hard to deal with, Madeline."

"What do you mean?" Madeline asked.

"I know that I've done and said things over the years that have hurt your feelings, but I want you to understand that it has come from a place of hurt, myself. I realize I should've seen a therapist after your father left. I just thought they were kind of silly at the time. But as the years have gone on and we drifted apart, I figured out that a lot of the problem, maybe all the problem, was me. I was hard to be around, even when I showed up here. Something about this little town has softened me a bit."

Madeline smiled slightly. "Are you saying that Jubilee has healed you?"

"Well, I wouldn't go too far. I'm getting better. I think I should talk to somebody about my feelings, and maybe some resentments I have toward your father and what happened there. It's made me a colder, more critical, more pessimistic person. And honestly, I didn't have a reason to do anything about it until I came here."

"I think it's great that you want to get help, Mom. You deserve to be happy."

"I pray you can forgive me for keeping this from you, and I hope that you'll still agree to help me through surgery, because nothing would make me happier than to have my daughter by my side."

"I will help you," Madeline said, reaching across the table and putting her hand over her mother's. "But from now on, you have to promise to tell me the truth, no matter how hard it is. And you have to also promise to try not to be so critical, try not to pick things apart."

"I'll try. I promise," she said.

"So, I guess we should finish eating, and maybe we can go into town to do some Christmas shopping?"

"That sounds like a lot of fun," Eloise said.

Frannie sat at the farmhouse table in her grandmother's kitchen, surrounded by a lifetime of memories. She was looking through old photographs, each one of them a snapshot frozen in time. Her fingers traced the edges of one picture of her grandmother, young and radiant with her whole life ahead of her, standing in front of the very house that Frannie now called home.

The weight of the legacy that she'd inherited sometimes sat on her shoulders, both as a responsibility and as a comfort. She continued looking through all the pictures of her grandmother as she got older, had children, and then eventually had a grandchild - Frannie.

There were even pictures of Frannie running through the hills behind the house. Those frolicking hills. It made Frannie smile to see them. As she was lost in her thoughts, she was startled by a knock at the front door. She stood up, putting the photograph back on the table, and walked through the living room to the front door. The wooden floorboards creaked beneath her feet. It was a familiar sound that made her always feel at home.

When she opened the door, she saw Cole standing on the porch holding two big grocery bags full of food, smiling.

"Hey, Frannie. I thought I might surprise you. Mind if I cook you dinner?"

Frannie's heart did a full flip in her chest. "Oh my gosh, I would love that. Come on in."

It was actually good timing because Frannie had been so busy with the bakery opening that she'd forgotten to go to the grocery store. All she had in the house was a half a carton of eggs and a couple of pieces of cheese. She'd planned to make herself an omelet for dinner if nothing else.

Cole stepped inside and walked toward the kitchen. He moved with a sense of familiarity because he'd been in this house many times when they were in high school. He set the bags on the kitchen counter, sighing with relief. "Whew!"

"It looks like you brought the whole store," Frannie joked, looking into the bags.

"Only the essentials for a perfect Italian dinner."

He laid out a box of spaghetti noodles, a big block of Parmesan cheese, a head of romaine lettuce for a side salad and a few other things, including a bottle of red wine and a baguette.

She watched him walk around the kitchen, pulling out pots and pans as if he lived there every day. He filled a pot with water and set it on the stove and then looked at her with a smile.

"What I want you to do is sit and relax while I prepare the dinner. Does that sound good?"

She smiled and sat down at the kitchen table again. "Actually, I think that sounds wonderful. I'm pretty exhausted, and you seem to have everything under control."

He laughed. "Okay, your highness. Then you sit there and enjoy because you now have the chef in the house."

She had no idea if he could cook or not. The last time they'd been on a date was when they were in high school, and for sure he wasn't a good cook then. She distinctly remembered eating macaroni and cheese with cut up hot dogs in it at his house.

She watched him as he moved around the kitchen, starting to prepare their dinner. He chopped and sauteed and before long, a mouthwatering aroma of garlic and simmering tomato sauce filled the space. For a moment, she allowed herself to imagine that they were happily married, cooking dinner for their kids in the other room.

"You know, this reminds me of that time we tried to cook dinner together in high school," he said. "Do you remember? We almost set the kitchen on fire at my house."

Frannie laughed. "Oh, I remember. Your mom got so mad at us, but she couldn't stop laughing. We were just two clueless teenagers trying to put out a grease fire with dish towels."

Cole chuckled as he stirred the sauce. "Yeah, I guess we've both come a long way since then. At least now I know I can make spaghetti without causing a disaster."

"We were so young, Cole, but it felt so serious, so real. I really thought we would be together forever."

He set the wooden spoon down and walked over to the table, sitting down across from her. "I did, too. As I said, I was young and stupid, and I thought we had to go separate ways. I guess when you're that young, you just can't see the forest for the trees."

"I suppose. We all make mistakes, especially at those young ages."

"I was a fool, Frannie. I let something good slip away because I was scared. Scared of failing you and my family."

"We were just kids. We didn't know any better."

"True, but some things you never forget, like the way you looked on our first date with that red sweater and those tight blue jeans."

She waved her hand at him. "Cole."

"I always remembered the sound of your laughter or how it felt when I would hold you close or when we would slow dance at our school dances. Those are the memories that stay with you no matter where life takes you." Before she could respond, he stood up and walked back to the stove, turning off the heat. The rich aroma of tomatoes and herbs filled the air. "Are you ready?"

“Absolutely. I'm starving," she said, standing up. She walked over to the stove where he handed her a plate with a big pile of noodles. He ladled sauce over the cooked spaghetti.

"You know, cooking for someone has always felt like a way to show love without words.”

"I can see that. There is something intimate about it, isn't there? Sharing a meal that you've made with your own hands?"

Cole took both plates and carried them to the table. "Yeah, it's like giving someone a part of yourself, in a way." They sat down across from each other, silence filling the air for a few minutes. "Do you remember our senior prom?" Cole said after taking his first bite.

She laughed, "How could I forget? You in that rented tux looking so incredibly uncomfortable, but so handsome."

"And you were breathtaking," Cole said softly. "I remember thinking I was the luckiest guy in the world to be there with Frannie Franklin."

She felt her cheeks warm at the compliment. "I felt the same way."

"I thought about that night a lot over the years,

about how it felt to dance with you, to hold you close, and I always wondered what would've happened if I had just never let go."

"It's hard, isn't it? Wondering about the what ifs?"

He reached across the table, touching her hand. "It is, but we're here now Frannie, and that's what matters. For some reason, we've been given a second chance, and I don't plan on wasting it."

"Neither do I, Cole. Neither do I."

Madeline sat next to her mother in the sterile, softly lit doctor's office. She could tell that her mother was nervous. Having surgery at any age was scary, but Eloise had confided in her that she was a little worried about having it in her seventies. She'd heard horror stories from some of her friends who said that their spouses or other loved ones had never been the same after a surgery.

The tension between them had eased a lot since their emotional conversation, but today was a big day. Madeline was going to meet her mother's doctor, talk about her upcoming knee surgery, and learn about what recovery would entail. Dr.

Williams walked into the room holding a medical chart.

"Hello, Eloise. This must be your daughter, Madeline."

"Yes. Nice to meet you," Madeline said, reaching out and shaking his hand.

"Thank you both for coming in. Eloise, how are you feeling today?"

"I'm anxious to get this over with," she said, smiling slightly. Madeline reached over and squeezed her mother's hand.

"We're ready to hear what you have to say, Dr. Williams."

Madeline was thankful that her mother had found a doctor so close to Jubilee. She must have done a lot of investigation to find him since she hadn't ever been to Jubilee before. It made her realize just how much her mother wanted her to take care of her after surgery.

"All right, then let's get to it. Eloise, as I explained to you, you have what's called osteoarthritis in your knee. This is a degenerative condition, meaning it's only going to get worse over time. The cartilage that cushions the bones wears away, and it causes the pain you're having, and sometimes stiffness."

"Yes, I've been feeling it for years, but it's just

gotten unbearable recently. My doctor back home has been giving me injections in my knee."

"That's often how it goes. Now, the surgery that we're proposing is a total knee replacement. We'll remove the damaged bone and the cartilage. Then we'll replace it with an artificial joint. This joint is made of metal and high grade plastic. It will allow for smoother movement and a lot less pain."

"And the recovery?" Madeline asked.

"Oh yes, the recovery. Well, you'll be in the hospital for a few days. We want to monitor you. After that, you're going to need physical therapy to get your strength and mobility back. During that time, you're going to require assistance with daily activities for a short while, possibly bathing and dressing, that sort of thing."

"I'll be there, Mom. You won't go through this alone," Madeline said.

"Thank you, dear."

"It's good that you have support. Family is critical during times like these."

"We'll get through this one step at a time."

“Well, I'm very happy that I get to enjoy the holidays before I have to start recovering from surgery."

"Yes, you'll absolutely get to enjoy the holidays," Dr. Williams said. "And don't worry. I think you're in pretty good health, so recovery should be without complication. If anything comes up, we'll deal with it at that time."

As they finished up the appointment and walked out to the car, Madeline felt a sense of gratitude that she got to be there for her mother, that they were getting this second chance at a brand new relationship. Like the many times her mother had taken care of her when she had the flu or a skinned knee, Madeline would take good care of her mother.

Frannie looked up from the counter where she was rearranging a fresh batch of blueberry muffins. She smiled when she saw Geneva and Perky walk in.

"Good morning, you two. What brings you here so early?" Frannie asked, wiping her hands on her apron.

"Well, we heard somebody's been baking up a storm, and we just couldn't resist a little sugar in the morning," Geneva said.

"And I've been craving one of those cranberry-orange scones all morning," Perky said.

Frannie laughed. "Well, you're both in luck. I just

took a batch out of the oven. I have some fresh coffee, so have a seat. I'll bring them over."

Geneva and Perky sat down at a table near the window where the morning light streamed in. The bakery was a cozy haven, with its walls adorned with vintage baking tools and framed recipes written in cursive. There was a chalkboard menu that hung above the counter, and the air was filled with the comforting aroma of baked goods and brewing coffee. Frannie walked over and joined them, as she had a lull in customers at that moment. She had a steaming plate of scones and two cups of coffee.

"Here we go. Fresh from the oven."

"Oh, these look great," Geneva said, picking up a scone and taking a bite. "They are just heavenly. You've got the magic touch like your grandmother, Frannie."

"These are perfect," Perky said.

Frannie's cheeks blushed. "Thank you. It always means the world to me to know that people are enjoying what I bake. So, what's going on with you two?"

"We should be asking you that," Geneva said, her eyes twinkling mischievously. "The word around town is that you and Cole have been spending quite a lot of time together recently."

"Well, yes, we have."

"Do tell. We want all the details," Perky said, leaning in.

Frannie hesitated for a moment, but she just couldn't resist. "Okay, so he came over the other night, unexpectedly, with groceries in his arms, and he cooked dinner for me at my nana's house. It was so romantic."

"Oh, that sounds incredibly sweet," Geneva said.

"It was. We spent the whole evening talking about high school and the first time we fell in love, and it was just nice. Comfortable. You know?"

"And, did you kiss? Come on, spill the beans," Perky said.

Frannie laughed. "No, we didn't kiss. Well, unless you count the kiss on the cheek he gave me at the door before he left. We're taking things slowly. After all, we do have a lot of history. We just don't want to rush into anything."

"Slow and steady wins the race, especially when it comes to matters of the heart," Geneva said nodding her head.

"All right, but you better keep us updated. We are living vicariously through you, you know," Perky said.

Frannie stared at her. "You know that you've been married for fifty years, right?"

Perky laughed. "Yes. And when you've been married for fifty years, you can tell me just how romantic things are."

Geneva giggled. "Well, just keep us up to date if you need any grandmotherly type advice."

"I promise. You two will be the first to know if anything significant happens," Frannie said, rolling her eyes and laughing.

They continued chatting and savoring the scones for a few more minutes before another customer came in, and Frannie had to get up and take care of them. She waved goodbye to Geneva and Perky and went back to running her new successful bakery.

CHAPTER 14

Madeline's car traveled along the winding mountain road. The scenery outside was a mixture of trees that were still green, even in winter, and others that had lost their leaves completely. The trees on the tops of the mountains were dusted with the first snow of the season.

She looked over at her mother, who seemed to be lost in thought after the doctor appointment about her knee surgery.

"Hey, Mom, do you mind if we make a quick stop?" Madeline asked, pointing to a scenic overlook they were just about to pass.

"Of course not, dear."

Madeline pulled in and parked the car. Both of them stepped out, wrapping their coats tightly around them. The overlook promised a stunning view of the valley below, and the small town of Jubilee was nestled among the hills like a hidden gem.

"You know, I stopped here not long after I moved to Jubilee," Madeline said, her eyes scanning over the horizon. "I got caught in a pop-up thunderstorm, and as if that wasn't bad enough, I managed to lock myself out of my car."

Eloise laughed. "Oh, Madeline, only you could manage that. You really were like a fish out of water."

"I know, right? I had to flag down this older gentleman who was driving by in probably the oldest truck I had ever seen, but thankfully he helped me get my car unlocked. He took me back to his house and called a friend that had a tow truck, but it was quite the adventure."

"Well, at least it sounds like you've made some great memories here."

"I have, Mom. I really have. And I'm so excited about the future, and all the memories I'm going to get to make with Brady, Jasmine, and Anna especially."

They stood there in silence for a moment. "You know, sometimes I think back to the days I had with your father, and I have regrets."

"What do you mean?"

"I just sometimes wonder if I could have done more to keep him from leaving us like he did. I feel like I missed out on a lifetime of memories I could've had."

Madeline shook her head. "That was his fault, Mom. No matter what, you don't cheat on your spouse. You work through things or you divorce, but you don't cheat on someone and then leave your child behind like he did."

"Well, it doesn't mean I don't sometimes just think about what could have been."

Madeline felt sorry for her mom in that moment as she stared out over the mountains, looking at all the years behind her. All those years without love in her life, and many years without her own daughter.

"So, what are you thinking about doing after surgery? Going back home? Staying in Jubilee?"

"Well, I've been thinking about that a lot, actually. I'm not sure. When I'm back at home, it's a lonely place, even though I'm surrounded by people."

Madeline took in a deep breath before speaking. "You know, you could always stay here with me. I have plenty of room."

"Are you sure? I wouldn't want to impose, Madeline. I mean, we haven't had the best relationship until recently."

"It's not an imposition, Mom. It's an invitation, and it's an open one."

Eloise looked back out over the mountains. "It is a big decision."

"I know it is, but as I have found out myself, sometimes big decisions are what lead you to beautiful new chapters."

"You always had a way with words, my dear."

"Think about it, okay? No pressure. Just know that you're welcome in my home and in my life."

"I will think about it, Madeline. I promise, I will."

A few moments later, they got back into the car, and Madeline made a different turn than she had expected.

"Do you mind if we make one more stop?"

"Sure, dear. You're the one driving. It's not like I can say anything."

"Well, you're not a prisoner," Madeline said, laughing.

"Where are we going?"

"Well, there's somebody I'd like you to meet."

"Oh, who's that?"

"You'll see," Madeline said as she turned into the parking lot of the local park.

When they got out of the car, she led her mom down a small path that opened up to a pond. The surface was starting to freeze over because it was getting so cold. Near the pond stood an older man with a white beard scattering birdseed around him. It was Burt, one of her favorite people she'd met in Jubilee so far. He held out his hand and birds landed on him, eating the seeds from his hand.

"Hey, Burt," Madeline called out as they approached.

"Ah, Madeline. How are you?"

"I'm good. Thank you. I just wanted you to meet my mom, Eloise. Mom, this is Burt. He's a local sage and wizard around here, friend to all creatures."

Burt laughed. "Pleased to meet you, ma'am."

Eloise shook his hand. "Well, the pleasure is mine. Madeline has mentioned to me that there was an interesting fellow at the park who fed the animals."

"Would you like to try?"

"Me?"

"Yes. It's not hard."

"I don't know if they would eat out of my hand," Eloise said, her voice shaking a little as she laughed.

"Sure they will. Come over here."

Eloise walked over and sat down on a small park

bench near the edge of the water. Burt sat beside her and put birdseed in her hand. "Now just hold your hand up as still as you can, and you'll be surprised at what happens."

Eloise smiled and held her hand in the air. A few moments later, a little bird came down from the tree nearby and landed on her fingertips, eating the seeds in her hand. Eloise's eyes widened as she giggled like a young girl. "Oh, my goodness."

"It's pretty magical, isn't it?" Burt said.

"It really is. And you feed the squirrels too?" she asked as the little bird flew away.

"Of course. They like peanuts. All you have to do is kneel down."

"Oh, I don't think I can do that right now," Eloise said, laughing. "I need to have knee surgery right after Christmas."

"Oh, goodness. I had that a few years ago. It's a bit of a tough recovery, but you'll feel better than ever once you're over the worst of it."

"Well, I'm glad to hear you had good success with it."

Madeline stood back further away and watched the two of them chatting. Just as she had thought, these two would get along well. She hoped that if Eloise found a friend nearby, she would be more willing to get out in Jubilee and live with her. It would be nice to know her mother had some kind of life. Back at the retirement community, it didn't sound like she was doing that at all.

"Well, it's getting cold. Burt, are you going to stay out here?" Madeline asked.

"Somebody's got to feed the animals. I'll go in a bit."

"Well, keep warm. Mom, I think we should get home."

"I think you're right. It was so nice to meet you, Burt."

"It was very nice to meet you, Eloise. I do hope you'll come back and feed the animals with me one day."

She smiled. "Thank you for the invitation. I may just take you up on that."

As they walked away, Madeline said nothing but kept glancing over at her mother, who had a large grin on her face as they walked to the car. Oh, yes, Eloise had a little crush. That much was sure.

It was a crisp December morning, just a couple of weeks before Christmas, and the sky was an icy, clear blue. Frannie and Cole set up a couple of folding chairs right in front of the bakery, which was already buzzing with the smell of fresh baked gingerbread cookies and peppermint mochas that Perky had brought over. They had a string of twinkling fairy lights on the bakery's window, which cast a warm glow.

"Do you think we've got the best seats in the house?" Cole asked, pulling a blanket over both of them.

"Absolutely. We've got some prime real estate right here."

"Are you excited to see the Jubilee Christmas parade again?"

"More than you can imagine. I only got to go to a couple of them when I was in high school, and I didn't appreciate that sort of thing back then."

Frannie looked at the crowd forming around the square. There were families starting to line the streets, children bundled up in their puffy coats, their faces flushed red with anticipation.

"Jubilee has a way of making every event feel like a big family gathering," Cole said.

"It does. I never knew how much I missed community until I came back here."

Perky and her husband, Eddie, walked by. Eddie was holding the leash of their small white dog. "Morning, you two. Are you saving us any seats for this parade?"

"Of course," Frannie said, waving them over. "Want some hot chocolate? I just made a fresh batch in there. Or, of course, you can have one of your peppermint mochas."

"You know, I don't mind if we do. I'd love some hot chocolate," Perky said.

Cole went inside to get the drinks, and Frannie and Perky chatted about the parade's lineup. "I hear that the high school marching band has a new routine, and you know there's going to be a float for the local animal shelter. They have a bunch of dogs dressed up like they live at the North Pole," Perky said, giggling.

"Well, that sounds just adorable," Frannie said. "And how are you doing, Eddie?"

"Oh, I'm doing fair to middling," Eddie said. He was always a man of few words.

Cole returned with a tray of hot chocolates complete with whipped cream on top and a little sprinkle of cinnamon.

"Here we go. Enjoy your liquid warmth."

Perky and Eddie opened up their two chairs right beside Frannie and Cole and sat down. They all sipped their drinks, listening to the distant sounds of jingling bells and marching drums. The parade was definitely about to start.

"Here we go," Eddie announced, as the first float turned the corner. It was a winter wonderland scene that had a snow machine that showered the crowd with fluffy white snowflakes. Frannie felt a sense of childlike wonder wash over her. She glanced over at Cole, who was watching the parade. She thought about the future. What if they got married and had children and one day they got to bring their own kids to the Jubilee Christmas Parade? It almost made her eyes fill with tears. He turned to look at her almost as if he sensed that she was looking at him. And for a moment, they held each other's gaze surrounded by the magic of the season, and then each of them turned back to the parade.

Madeline sat on the edge of her folding chair, her eyes scanning each float in the parade as it meandered down Main Street. She was sitting between Geneva, who was wrapped in a green and red plaid shawl, and Jasmine, who had Anna sitting on her lap. Anna was bundled up in a pink, puffy coat, her eyes wide with excitement as she held on to the small bag she was using to collect candy.

"Here comes the volunteer firefighter float," Jasmine said, pointing down the street. Brady was riding on that float today, and Anna was very impressed by it. She was so excited to see her uncle go by in the parade.

Every time Madeline saw Brady, her heart skipped a beat. She thought maybe she might have to see a cardiologist about that at some point. She couldn't help but feel a rush of pride and love as the float came into view, and she saw him standing near the back, dressed in his firefighter gear with a Santa hat sitting on top of his head. There was just something about a man in uniform, even if it included a Santa hat.

When Brady's eyes found hers, his face broke into a wide grin. He raised his hand up and waved at her and then shaped his hands into the sign for "I love you." Madeline felt her cheeks turn red as she returned the gesture.

"Look, Anna, there's Uncle Brady," Jasmine said.

But Anna was already on her feet, holding her bag in the air ready for more candy as if she needed it. As the float passed by their spot, Brady reached into a bucket of candy canes and tossed them by the handful in her direction. Anna squealed with delight as she caught one of them. Other kids rushed over and took several from the ground.

"Isn't he something?" Geneva said, nudging Madeline with her elbow. "That man looks at you like you're the star on top of the tallest Christmas tree."

Madeline laughed, feeling a warmth that didn't seem to have anything to do with the hot apple cider that she was currently drinking. "He does have a way of making me feel special. To be honest, I never thought I'd have this kind of love in my fifties."

"Well, he should make you feel special because you *are* special," Geneva said. "And this is a magical season, but you know, love is always the best gift of all."

Madeline nodded her head. She felt that to her core. She had never had a love in her life like she had with Brady. She watched as the float moved on down the street and waited for the next one to come behind. But she felt grateful, not just for Brady's love, but for the love she had found in this community and the love she had found from brand new friends and family. This was home, this was Christmas, and she couldn't imagine that life could ever get any better than this.

Having never had her own kids, Madeline had not been to a “Cookies with Santa” event, but today she found there was a first for everything. Brady, Anna and Madeline stepped into the town hall which had been transformed into a winter wonderland. There were twinkling lights everywhere, all different kinds of Christmas trees, and the scent of cinnamon and pine filled the air like a thick fog. A giant Christmas tree stood in the corner, its branches covered in ornaments and tinsel.

"Hey look, Anna. There's Santa," Brady said, pointing toward a corner where Santa Claus sat in a grand velvet-lined chair. There was a line of eager children waiting for their moment on Santa's lap.

Anna's eyes got big, her face lighting up like one of the Christmas trees. "Can we go? Please?"

"Of course," Madeline said. They waited in line with Anna fidgeting, her eyes never looking away from Santa Claus. Finally, it was her turn, and she climbed onto his lap, whispering whatever her Christmas wishes were into his ear. Madeline wondered what those were. After having such a tough year, she hoped that Anna got everything she wanted for Christmas. Madeline caught Brady's eye, and they shared a smile, both touched by the little girl's awe and wonder.

Anna finished with Santa and took a candy cane, and then they walked around the rest of the town hall. There was a place to pick up some Christmas cookies that other children had decorated, or you could decorate your own. Anna decided to decorate her own, of course, so Madeline and Brady waited a few moments while she did that, and then each of them stuffed their faces with the giant icing-filled Christmas cookie. Then, they walked back out onto the town square where the festival was going on.

"There is nothing like live music to get you in the Christmas spirit," Brady said, pulling Madeline closer, his arm around her.

“I love Christmas music,” Madeline said.

They listened to a jazzy rendition of Jingle Bells, and she thought that Brady might just break out into a dance. She nodded and looked around at all the families laughing and talking, the little kids dancing and twirling around, couples holding hands. It seemed like a scene straight out of one of those sappy TV Christmas movies, and she couldn't have been happier to be a part of it. She realized that she was currently living her own sappy TV Christmas movie.

"Want to grab some hot chocolate?" Brady asked, leading them over to the hot chocolate stand, which was adorable. It looked like a little bakery on wheels, and the aroma was intoxicating. Madeline had already filled herself with hot apple cider and now she was going to do the same with hot chocolate. She was going to have a sugar buzz that wouldn't end for days. But as she took a sip, the warmth spread through her. It was a cold December day in the mountains, and a warm drink did just the trick.

When they finished enjoying their hot chocolate, they wandered over to the live nativity scene. There were local volunteers dressed as Joseph, Mary, and the wise men, and they had a baby doll that was swaddled up in the manger. It was far too cold to have a real baby playing the part.

"It's beautiful, isn't it," Madeline said.

"It really is. It's so easy to get caught up in the hustle and bustle of the season, but this is what it's really about when you think about it."

Madeline looked up at him, her eyes meeting his.

They were surrounded by the magic of Christmas and the people they loved, and she was feeling so peaceful today. "I'm so glad that I get to share this with you."

Brady leaned down and kissed her softly. "And there's no one else in the world I'd rather share it with."

As they stood there hand in hand, they watched Anna run off to join some other children making snow angels in the fake snow that had been spread across the town square, Madeline knew that this would be a Christmas to remember. Her first one in Jubilee and possibly the best one she'd ever had.

CHAPTER 15

It was time for the lighting of the Jubilee Christmas tree right in the center of the town square. And as Frannie stood next to Cole, she couldn't believe where she was right now. Just a couple of months ago, she never could have imagined that she'd even be in Jubilee at all, much less living in her grandmother's home, running her own bakery, and rekindling things with the love of her life. It seemed like she'd been walking through a dream until right now, just before they were about to light the Christmas tree, when she could feel the electricity standing so close to him.

As the crowd gathered around the town square, everybody's faces lit up by the soft glow of street lamps and twinkling lights, she felt like there was so much to be excited for in the future. The mayor took the stage, standing next to the honorary mayor, Murphy the dog. He thanked everyone for coming and spoke to them briefly about the spirit of community and the magic of Christmas. He said a prayer and then counted down from three, and Frannie suddenly felt Cole's hand find hers, their fingers intertwining naturally.

"3, 2, 1…" the mayor shouted, followed by a loud bark from Murphy. In that moment, the enormous tree burst into light, its branches adorned by thousands of twinkling bulbs and sparkling ornaments. Everybody cheered, but all Frannie could focus on was the handsome man standing beside her. As if they were pulled by some universal magnetic force, their eyes met. Cole's gaze was intense, filled with a mixture of emotion that Frannie could feel deep in her own soul. And as if time stood still, the crowd suddenly went silent around them. It was just a hum in the background.

"Frannie," Cole whispered, "I've been wanting to do this since the moment I saw you again." And before she could say anything, he leaned in, his lips meeting hers in a kiss that was tender and yet passionate. It was as if all the years they'd been apart just collapsed onto each other. All the words left unsaid were channeled into that single perfect moment.

When they pulled away, Frannie felt a sense of completeness that she hadn't in years. Maybe she'd never felt it. She looked up at Cole, his eyes shining brighter than any of the lights on the town Christmas tree. "That was..." she started, lost for words.

"Long overdue," he said.

Frannie nodded, smiling. "Very long overdue."

As the night wore on, Madeline was exhausted and honestly ready to go home, but she had promised to go caroling with a group of people in town. She felt a sense of excitement because it was something she'd never done before. She bundled up in her warmest coat, a red scarf wrapped snugly around her neck. Brady looked festive in his Santa hat, and they smiled as they joined Geneva, Jasmine, and a small group from Geneva's church on the town square.

"Are we all ready to spread some Christmas cheer?" Geneva called to the group. She was the unofficial leader, but her voice was strong, and everybody followed Geneva no matter what. Everybody yelled "yes" and "absolutely." And with that, they all set off around the square and down some of the side streets to the houses. The group was a mixture of ages from younger children to senior citizens, all dressed in festive attire, their breath visible in the chilly air. They walked and sang, their voices harmonizing beautifully.

The first stop was on the square where families were still enjoying the end of the festival. Madeline saw all the faces of young and old who smiled as they listened while the group sang Jingle Bells and Silent Night. Sometimes the crowd joined in, their voices filling the space of the square.

"Isn't this amazing?" Jasmine said, smiling at Madeline between songs. "I've never been caroling before."

Madeline smiled. "Neither have I. It's like stepping into some kind of sappy Christmas movie. In fact, this whole day has been like that."

"I used to think those movies were sort of silly when I'd watch them on TV at Christmas." Jasmine said. "But now I get it. I get why people want to live in a world like that where every day is happy and everyone wants to help each other."

After they left the square, they made their way

down some of the side streets stopping at different homes. Each time, people would appear on their front porches, grinning from ear to ear as they listened to the Christmas music. One elderly woman even had tears in her eyes as she thanked them for stopping by.

"This is the first time I've had carolers in years," she said, her voice shaky. "Thank you for bringing some Christmas spirit to my home."

When they walked away, Brady mentioned that he hadn't seen a Christmas tree in the woman's house, and that he was planning to bring some of his volunteer firefighter friends over there the next day to make sure that the woman had Christmas cheer in her home for the rest of the month of December. Madeline felt many lumps in her throat as the evening progressed. It was the moments like these that made her so grateful for Jubilee, this community that seemed to be one of a kind.

As they continued, she looked at Brady, her most cherished person in the world. They sang Let It Snow, and he put his arm around her, pulling her close, and she felt the comforting peace that she always felt being with him. Sometimes she thought about the years she was married to Jacob and how she'd never felt that kind of love. She honestly hadn't believed it existed, and that it was just a fairytale like what she wrote in her books. Now, she knew it was real.

They stopped at a home where a young couple lived. The woman was pregnant, and her husband was looking at her with so much love that it made Madeline think about her own future, what her life would be like with Brady.

They sang her favorite Christmas song, O Holy Night. And when they hit the high notes, she felt as if the entire world stood still, like a magical moment was happening.

Finally, they got back to the square, Madeline's voice exhausted and her body right along with it. They saw Eloise sitting with Anna, both of them wrapped up in blankets. They sang their last song in front of them - We Wish You a Merry Christmas - and Madeline saw that her mother was singing along with a genuine smile on her face. As everyone dispersed and headed to their cars, Madeline climbed into Brady's truck, sitting snugly against him while her mother got into Geneva's much lower car. There was no way she could climb into Brady's truck with her bum knee.

"This was the best caroling event I think we've

ever had," Geneva said, talking to them through the window. "Thank you for being a part of it."

Madeline smiled and waved. "Thank you, Geneva. This is exactly what I needed." This is what the holidays were about: community, love and the simple joy of spending time with people on a cold winter's night.

The scent of gingerbread was wafting through Madeline's cabin, mingling with the freshly brewed coffee she had on the kitchen counter, as the Christmas tree twinkled in the corner and cast a beautiful glow over the room. Madeline looked around at the faces of Brady, Eloise, Jasmine and Anna.

"Okay, everybody. Are we going to start our official first annual gingerbread house contest?" Madeline announced.

"Yes!" they all yelled. Everyone had a gingerbread house kit in front of them, complete with gum drops, peppermints, and all different colors of icing.

"Okay. So, remember we're posting the pictures of our gingerbread houses on social media, and we're going to let our friends vote for the winner without knowing who did which one," Jasmine said, her phone at the ready. "Everybody has thirty minutes to work on theirs, and then we're going to post the pictures."

They all frantically started assembling their gingerbread houses. There were a lot of cries of "oops" and "whoops" as they worked on their houses. Sometimes a wall would cave in or a roof would slide off. Anna, of course, was the most animated, meticulously placing gumdrops on her rooftop. Brady, who was an outdoorsman at heart, was really trying to create a gingerbread barn with little animal shaped candies.

"What do you think?" he asked Madeline as he held up a gummy bear that was supposed to look like a cow.

"It's creative, I guess," Madeline said, laughing.

Eloise was surprisingly engrossed in her project, her eyes narrow in concentration. She was carefully piping designs on the walls of the house, her hands surprisingly steady. "You're really into this, aren't you, Mom?"

Eloise smiled. "I haven't done something like this in many years. It's actually fun."

After thirty minutes had passed, Jasmine called time, and each person arranged their gingerbread house on the table to make sure that they could capture it from various angles in the pictures. Then she snapped a group photo of everybody standing in front of the table full of houses.

"Everybody say gingerbread," she said, snapping the photo. Madeline uploaded the photos of the gingerbread houses to her social media and then set up a poll for her friends to vote. She gave them one hour. As they waited for the votes to come in, they all sipped on coffee and nibbled on Christmas cookies that Madeline and Anna had made earlier in the day. Anna enjoyed a big mug of hot chocolate covered in whipped cream and sprinkles. Madeline finally felt the timer go off on her phone and decided to go check the poll results.

"And the winner is... Oh my gosh, Mom. You won!"

Eloise's eyes widened. "Really? Oh, my goodness. I haven't won anything in many years."

Anna clapped. "Your house is really pretty, Grandma Eloise."

Eloise beamed. "Thank you, Anna. Thank you, everybody, for such a fun evening. This has turned out to be one of the best Christmases I think I've ever had."

Madeline felt her eyes start to mist over as she

looked at her mother, realizing not only how far she'd come, but how far they had come in their relationship in the weeks that she'd been here. As they started to clean up and wrap the winning gingerbread house in plastic wrap, because Eloise declared she was going to keep it as a keepsake, Madeline watched her mother, her heart filled with love and gratitude knowing that she was getting a fresh new start, and that was the best Christmas present of all.

Frannie was becoming more and more at home in her grandmother's house. She had decorated it for Christmas, and tonight she had the fire lit and it really felt like home. *Her* home. She had cinnamon scented candles that she'd lit earlier, and the Christmas tree stood in the corner, casting twinkling lights all over the living room. Ornaments adorned the tree that held great memories for her. She'd found two boxes of old family ornaments up in the attic, and she was so thankful to have them.

Cole had arrived, and they sat down on the sofa and draped a soft blanket over themselves. A bowl of popcorn sat on the coffee table and two mugs of steaming hot chocolate with whipped cream and a sprinkle of cocoa powder sat beside them on the end table. Frannie had picked out one of her favorite Christmas movies. It was a heartwarming romantic comedy that she'd seen many times but she never tired of.

As the opening credits started to roll, she looked over at Cole, who was smiling.

"This is nice," he said.

"It really is."

She had been through so much over the last few years: a divorce, a career change, the loss of her grandmother, opening her own bakery. But now that she was sitting here with Cole, she felt such a sense of happiness, something she hadn't felt in a long time.

As the movie played and they laughed at the funny parts, Frannie sighed at the romantic scenes. Every so often, they would look over at each other, a silly grin on their faces. About halfway through the movie, there was a particularly touching scene. Cole turned to her.

“I know this might sound really cheesy, but it's moments like this that make me realize how much I have missed you, Frannie. And it also makes me realize how much I'm falling for you all over again."

"I've missed you too, Cole, and I'm falling for you, too. It scares me a little, if I'm honest."

He squeezed her hand. "It scares me too, but you know it's a good kind of scared. It's the kind that makes you want to take a chance on something that could be absolutely amazing."

"Exactly," she said, her heart pounding in her chest.

He leaned in closer and she felt her breath catch as their lips met in a sweet lingering kiss. It was a simple gesture, but it spoke volumes. As they pulled apart, she snuggled her head onto his shoulder, and they continued watching the movie. The feeling of happiness that she felt was something she hadn't experienced in years, probably since the last time her lips met Cole's. It was like everything was falling into place, the perfect ending to a Christmas movie.

As Madeline and Eloise stood in the old stone church in Jubilee, Madeline was excited to experience her first Christmas Eve candlelight service. She and her mother had come alone as Brady and Jasmine were preparing Anna's Christmas morning gifts from Santa.

They walked up the cobblestone path, arm in arm, their breath visible in the cold winter air. When they entered, they were greeted by the scent of evergreen and the soft melodies of Christmas hymns being played on an old piano. They found a pew near the back, settling in as the congregation continued to fill the sanctuary. Eloise scanned the crowd, her eyes taking in the beautiful stained-glass windows that depicted scenes from the nativity.

The service began, and the pastor spoke about the meaning of Christmas, the birth of hope, and the importance of community and family. Madeline felt her mother reach over and take her hand, their fingers intertwining. It was the simplest of gestures between mother and daughter, but it was unusual, and Madeline was grateful for it. When it came time for the candlelight portion of the service, the lights in the sanctuary dimmed and the ushers distributed candles to everyone. Each person on the end of the pew lit their candle from the usher's flame and then turned to light the person next to them. The pastor encouraged everyone to reflect on the light that they bring into the lives to those around them.

Eloise looked at her daughter and whispered, "You've brought so much light into my life, Madeline. I know I haven't always been good at showing it, but

I'm so proud of the woman that you've become and the life that you've built for yourself."

"Thank you, Mom. That means everything to me. And I'm proud of how much you've changed and evolved just in the last few weeks that you've been here."

"You know, I've been doing some thinking, and if the offer still stands, I'd like to take you up on it. I would like to live with you here in Jubilee."

Madeline was surprised. "Really? You want to stay?"

"I do. I found something here that I didn't even know was missing in my life. I thought I was home at the retirement community, but I realized I wasn't really living. I needed a community, and I found that here with you, my daughter."

"I would love for you to stay, Mom, more than anything in the world."

As they stood there with their candles flickering in the dim sanctuary, Madeline felt like her life had really changed. Every time she thought she was finished changing, something else came along. All the years of misunderstandings and tension with her mother had seemingly melted away, warmed by the holiday spirit, and now all that was left was an unbreakable mother and daughter bond. They joined the rest of the congregation singing Silent Night, their voices all blending together. But Madeline couldn't help but feel that this was the most perfect and magical Christmas Eve she'd ever experienced.

Christmas morning in the mountains was something that was unmatched in Madeline's mind. They woke up to a thick fog hanging over the mountains, making them almost completely invisible. But as the sun peaked through the clouds, it burned off the fog, and they were left with the beautiful blue-tinged mountains in the background.

The morning sun was coming through the windows and cast a beautiful glow across the room. The Christmas tree stood like a beacon in the corner, surrounded by brightly wrapped gifts and big bags of toys that Santa Claus had left the night before. Brady had brought them over the night before after Anna had finally drifted off to sleep.

As Brady, Jasmine and Anna arrived, Madeline greeted them at the door with a big smile.

"Santa Claus came down my chimney last night!"

she said. Anna grinned and clapped her hands together. Since they were living in a trailer, Brady thought it might be better for Anna to have all the gifts delivered by Santa to Madeline's house so they could enjoy Christmas together in her much bigger living room.

The air was filled with the scent of cinnamon rolls that Madeline had got up and baked that morning, and her mother finished up the coffee. They were all dressed in their favorite Christmas pajamas just so that they could complete the scene. Brady wanted to pull Anna straight from bed and bring her to Madeline's just so that it would be authentic.

They sat down as Jasmine captured all the moments of Anna opening her presents. She took pictures on her phone that she would later post on social media, just like the proud mother she was.

Brady walked over and handed Madeline a small elegantly wrapped box. "For you, my lady," he said, his eyes meeting hers.

She opened the box to reveal a beautiful silver necklace with a pendant that was shaped like the mountains. "Oh my goodness, Brady, this is beautiful."

"It reminded me of you when I saw it. That first time you went hiking with Geneva and then with me. The first time that you said the mountains felt like home." He helped her fasten the necklace around her neck. "I always want you to have a piece of that to remember where your home is."

She felt her eyes well with tears. "I love it, and I love you," she said, leaning in for a kiss.

Eloise had been watching the exchange and cleared her throat to interrupt them. "I have something for you too, Madeline," she said. She handed her a present wrapped in bright red paper. Madeline unwrapped the gift to reveal a leather-bound journal and a fancy pen. "For your stories," Eloise said. "The ones that have already changed so many lives and the ones that are yet to come."

Madeline was speechless, touched by the fact that her mother had actually given her something that was related to her author business. "Thank you, Mom. This means more than you'll ever know."

As the morning went on and Anna moved on to her stocking, pulling out candy, new colored pencils and smaller toys, she grinned and yelled with each new gift. Jasmine laughed, taking pictures. Madeline looked around the room and wondered what the year to come was going to bring. All that she knew was that she got to do it with the people that she loved, and that was more than enough for her.

EPILOGUE

The sky was dark, only stars scattered across it, and a partial moon lit the frolicking hills behind Frannie's house. It was cool enough to need the fire pit on her porch. She looked over at Cole, a smile spreading across her face.

"You know, I can't believe it's almost a new year and how different my life is now. The bakery is doing so well, and I have reconnected with my high school sweetheart. What could be better?"

He reached over and held her hand. "I feel the same way. Although I'm here to take care of my dad, and that's hard at times, I feel so honored that I got to take over his business and continue his legacy. And I feel even more excited about our future, Frannie. I'm never going to leave your side again. I hope you know that. You can't get rid of me."

"You can't get rid of me either," she said, leaning over and kissing him on the cheek. It was New Year's Eve, and they were waiting for the fireworks to explode behind the hills.

"Well, either way, I can't believe that we're about to see a new year together after all these years. Time flies when you're falling in love," Cole said.

She felt her heart swell at the sound of him saying love. They had come so far since their high school days, each of them having faced their own challenges and heartaches over the years, but love brought them back together again. Just then, the first firework burst into the sky, the vibrant colors illuminating the dark Georgia night. More and more of them followed. Each one were more dazzling than the last, lighting up the mountains behind them.

"I don't know what this new year holds," Cole suddenly said, "but I do want to spend it with you. I want to spend all my New Years with you."

She felt her eyes well with tears at the sincerity. "I can't think of a better way to start the new year than to be sitting here with you in my grandmother's home."

When the clock struck midnight, bringing in the arrival of the new year, they stood and kissed in a way that was a promise and a prayer, a promise of loving each other forever, and a prayer for the happiness that awaited them in the future.

Brady and Madeline stood on her back deck overlooking the mountains. A freestanding propane heater stood next to them so they didn't freeze to death on this cold New Year's Eve. As they waited for the fireworks to begin, Madeline was excited about the new year ahead and all that it could hold for her and her friends and family. Eloise, who had just had knee surgery days before, was cozy in her bedroom, watching the New Year's Eve countdown on TV. Madeline leaned into Brady, resting her head on his shoulder.

"This year has certainly been a whirlwind."

He laughed. "That's one way to put it. Between your mom coming to town, you planning the Harvest Festival, cooking your first Thanksgiving dinner and all the Christmas activities, you've sure had your hands full."

"And let's not forget that I finished a book, and you've been running a farm and working as a volunteer firefighter, being a fantastic uncle... I think we should toast to those, to the most eventful year of our lives."

"The most eventful and the most wonderful," Brady said, clinking his glass of champagne against hers.

"And your house will be finished in just a couple of months," Madeline said.

"I can't wait for that. As much as I love living with my sister and Anna, that small trailer leaves a lot to be desired. We all need a bit more space. Anna is thrilled with the idea of having her own room to hang out and play with her toys."

Just then, the first firework exploded in the sky, its colors reflecting in their champagne glasses. Each one had more bursts of light and color than the one before it. Madeline looked over at Brady.

"You know, this year has taught me a lot about family and forgiveness and love. It's taught me about the kind of life I want to live, and I sure can't imagine ever living it without you."

"I feel the same way, Madeline. You have brought so much light into my life, and I can't wait to see what the future holds for us."

Inside, they could hear the countdown begin on TV. 10... 9... 8... then 3... 2... 1...

"Happy New Year!" could be heard from the TV

inside. The sky lit up with a grand finale of fireworks, but Brady and Madeline didn't seem to notice as he kissed her passionately, sealing their love and hopes for the future in one perfect moment. When they pulled apart, Madeline thought about how she couldn't even remember her last New Year's Eve, but she would never forget this one.

See a list of Rachel's other books at RachelHannaAuthor.com.

Made in United States
Orlando, FL
03 December 2023